W9-BAI-939

HUNGER

By KNUT HAMSUN

Translated by W. W. WORSTER

Introduction by
EDWIN BJÖRKMAN

Hunger
By Knut Hamsun
Translated by W. W. Worster
Introduction by Edwin Björkman

Print ISBN 13: 978-1-4209-6096-9
eBook ISBN 13: 978-1-4209-6016-7

This edition copyright © 2018. Digireads.com Publishing.

All rights reserved. No part of this publication may be reproduced, distributed, or transmitted in any form or by any means, including photocopying, recording, or other electronic or mechanical methods, without the prior written permission of the publisher, except in the case of brief quotations embodied in critical reviews and certain other noncommercial uses permitted by copyright law.

Cover Image: a detail of "The Starving", c. 1886 (oil on canvas), by Henri Jules Jean Geoffroy (1853-1924) / Museo Civico Revoltella, Trieste, Italy / Bridgeman Images.

Please visit *www.digireads.com*

Introduction

Since the death of Ibsen and Strindberg, Hamsun is undoubtedly the foremost creative writer of the Scandinavian countries. Those approaching most nearly to his position are probably Selma Lagerlöf in Sweden and Henrik Pontoppidan in Denmark. Both these, however, seem to have less than he of that width of outlook, validity of interpretation and authority of tone that made the greater masters what they were.

His reputation is not confined to his own country or the two Scandinavian sister nations. It spread long ago over the rest of Europe, taking deepest roots in Russia, where several editions of his collected works have already appeared, and where he is spoken of as the equal of Tolstoy and Dostoyevsky. The enthusiasm of this approval is a characteristic symptom that throws interesting light on Russia as well as on Hamsun.

Hearing of it, one might expect him to prove a man of the masses, full of keen social consciousness. Instead, he must be classed as an individualistic romanticist and a highly subjective aristocrat, whose foremost passion in life is violent, defiant deviation from everything average and ordinary. He fears and flouts the dominance of the many, and his heroes, who are nothing but slightly varied images of himself, are invariably marked by an originality of speech and action that brings them close to, if not across, the borderline of the eccentric.

In all the literature known to me, there is no writer who appears more ruthlessly and fearlessly himself, and the self thus presented to us is as paradoxical and rebellious as it is poetic and picturesque. Such a nature, one would think, must be the final blossoming of powerful hereditary tendencies, converging silently through numerous generations to its predestined climax. All we know is that Hamsun's forebears were sturdy Norwegian peasant folk, said only to be differentiated from their neighbours by certain artistic preoccupations that turned one or two of them into skilled craftsmen. More certain it is that what may or may not have been innate was favoured and fostered and exaggerated by physical environment and early social experiences.

Hamsun was born on Aug. 4, 1860, in one of the sunny valleys of central Norway. From there his parents moved when he was only four to settle in the far northern district of Lofoden—that land of extremes, where the year, and not the day, is evenly divided between darkness and light; where winter is a long dreamless sleep, and summer a passionate dream without sleep; where land and sea meet and intermingle so gigantically that man is all but crushed between the two—or else raised to titanic measures by the spectacle of their struggle.

The Northland, with its glaring lights and black shadows, its unearthly joys and abysmal despairs, is present and dominant in every line that Hamsun ever wrote. In that country his best tales and dramas are laid. By that country his heroes are stamped wherever they roam. Out of that country they draw their principal claims to probability. Only in that country do they seem quite at home. Today we know, however, that the pathological case represents nothing but an extension of perfectly normal tendencies. In the same way we know that the miraculous atmosphere of the Northland serves merely to develop and emphasize traits that lie slumbering in men and women everywhere. And on this basis the fantastic figures created by Hamsun relate themselves to ordinary humanity as the microscopic enlargement of a cross section to the living tissues. What we see is true in everything but proportion.

The artist and the vagabond seem equally to have been in the blood of Hamsun from the very start. Apprenticed to a shoemaker, he used his scant savings to arrange for the private printing of a long poem and a short novel produced at the age of eighteen, when he was still signing himself Knud Pedersen Hamsund. This done, he abruptly quit his apprenticeship and entered on that period of restless roving through trades and continents which lasted until his first real artistic achievement with "Hunger," In 1888-90. It has often been noted that practically every one of Hamsun's heroes is of the same age as he was then, and that their creator takes particular pain to accentuate this fact. It is almost as if, during those days of feverish literary struggle, he had risen to heights where he saw things so clearly that no subsequent experience could add anything but occasional details.

Before he reached those heights, he had tried life as coal-heaver and school teacher, as road-mender and surveyor's attendant, as farm hand and streetcar conductor, as lecturer and free-lance journalist, as tourist and emigrant. Twice he visited this country during the middle eighties, working chiefly on the plains of North Dakota and in the streets of Chicago. Twice during that time he returned to his own country and passed through the experiences pictured in "Hunger," before, at last, he found his own literary self and thus also a hearing from the world at large. While here, he failed utterly to establish any sympathetic contact between himself and the new world, and his first book after his return in 1888 was a volume of studies named "The Spiritual Life of Modern America," which a prominent Norwegian critic once described as "a masterpiece of distorted criticism." But I own a copy of this book, the fly-leaf of which bears the following inscription in the author's autograph:

"A youthful work. It has ceased to represent my opinion of America.
May 28, 1903. Knut Hamsun."

In its original form, "Hunger" was merely a sketch, and as such it appeared in 1888 in a Danish literary periodical, "New Earth." It attracted immediate widespread attention to the author, both on account of its unusual theme and striking form. It was a new kind of realism that had nothing to do with photographic reproduction of details. It was a professedly psychological study that had about as much in common with the old-fashioned conceptions of man's mental activities as the delirious utterances of a fever patient. It was life, but presented in the Impressionistic temper of a Gauguin or Cezanne. On the appearance of the completed novel in 1890, Hamsun was greeted as one of the chief heralds of the neo-romantlc movement then spreading rapidly through the Scandinavian north and finding typical expressions not only in the works of theretofore unknown writers, but in the changed moods of masters like Ibsen and Bjornson and Strindberg.

It was followed two years later by "Mysteries," which pretends to be a novel, but which may be better described as a delightfully irresponsible and defiantly subjective roaming through any highway or byway of life or letters that happened to take the author's fancy at the moment of writing. Some one has said of that book that in its abrupt swingings from laughter to tears, from irreverence to awe, from the ridiculous to the sublime, one finds the spirits of Dostoyevsky and Mark Twain blended.

The novels "Editor Lynge" and "New Earth," both published in 1893, were social studies of Christiania's Bohemia and chiefly characterized by their violent attacks on the men and women exercising the profession which Hamsun had just made his own. Then came "Pan" in 1894, and the real Hamsun, the Hamsun who ever since has moved logically and with increasing authority to "The Growth of the Soil," stood finally revealed. It is a novel of the Northland, almost without a plot, and having its chief interest in a primitively spontaneous man's reactions to a nature so overwhelming that it makes mere purposeless existence seem a sufficient end in itself. One may well question whether Hamsun has ever surpassed the purely lyrical mood of that book, into which he poured the ecstatic dreams of the little boy from the south as, for the first time, he saw the forestclad northern mountains bathing their feet in the ocean and their crowns in the light of a never-setting sun. It is a wonderful paean to untamed nature and to the forces let loose by it within the soul of man.

Like most of the great writers over there, Hamsun has not confined himself to one poetic mood or form, but has tried all of them. From the line of novels culminating in "Pan," he turned suddenly to the drama, and in 1895 appeared his first play, "At the Gates of the Kingdom." It was the opening drama of a trilogy and was followed by "The Game of Life" in 1896 and "Sunset Glow" in 1898. The first play is laid in

Christiania, the second in the Northland, and the third in Christiania again. The hero of all three is Ivar Kareno, a student and thinker who is first presented to us at the age of 29, then at 39, and finally at 50. His wife and several other characters accompany the central figure through the trilogy, of which the lesson seems to be that every one is a rebel at 30 and a renegade at 50. But when Kareno, the irreconcilable rebel of "At the Gates of the Kingdom," the heaven-storming truth-seeker of "The Game of Life," and the acclaimed radical leader in the first acts of "Sunset Glow," surrenders at last to the powers that be in order to gain a safe and sheltered harbor for his declining years, then another man of 29 stands ready to denounce him and to take up the rebel cry of youth to which he has become a traitor. Hamsun's ironical humor and whimsical manner of expression do more than the plot itself to knit the plays into an organic unit, and several of the characters are delightfully drawn, particularly the two women who play the greatest part in Kareno's life: his wife Eline, and Teresita, who is one more of his many feminine embodiments of the passionate and changeable Northland nature. Any attempt to give a political tendency to the trilogy must be held wasted. Characteristically, Kareno is a sort of Nietzschean rebel against the victorious majority, and Hamsun's seemingly cynical conclusions stress man's capacity for action rather than the purposes toward which that capacity may be directed.

Of three subsequent plays, "Vendt the Monk," (1903), "Queen Tamara" (1903) and "At the Mercy of Life" (1910), the first mentioned is by far the most remarkable. It is a verse drama in eight acts, centred about one of Hamsun's most typical vagabond heroes. The monk Vendt has much in common with Peer Gynt without being in any way an imitation or a duplicate. He is a dreamer in revolt against the world's alleged injustice, a rebel against the very powers that invisibly move the universe, and a passionate lover of life who in the end accepts it as a joyful battle and then dreams of the long peace to come. The vigor and charm of the verse proved a surprise to the critics when the play was published, as Hamsun until then had given no proof of any poetic gift in the narrower sense.

From 1897 to 1912 Hamsun produced a series of volumes that simply marked a further development of the tendencies shown in his first novels: "Siesta," short stories, 1897; "Victoria" a novel with a charming love story that embodies the tenderest note in his production, 1898; "In Wonderland," travelling sketches from the Caucasus, 1903; "Brushwood," short stories, 1903; "The Wild Choir," a collection of poems, 1904; "Dreamers," a novel, 1904; "Struggling Life," short stories and travelling sketches, 1905; "Beneath the Autumn Star" a novel, 1906; "Benoni," and "Rosa," two novels forming to some extent sequels to "Pan," 1908; "A Wanderer Plays with Muted Strings," a novel, 1909; and "The Last Joy," a shapeless work, half novel and half mere uncoordinated reflections, 1912.

The later part of this output seemed to indicate a lack of development, a failure to open up new vistas, that caused many to fear that the principal contributions of Hamsun already lay behind him. Then appeared in 1913 a big novel, "Children of the Time," which in many ways struck a new note, although led up to by "Rosa" and "Benoni." The horizon is now wider, the picture broader. There is still a central figure, and still he possesses many of the old Hamsun traits, but he has crossed the meridian at last and become an observer rather than a fighter and doer. Nor is he the central figure to the same extent as Lieutenant Glahn in "Pan" or Kareno in the trilogy. The life pictured is the life of a certain spot of ground—Segelfoss manor, and later the town of Segelfoss—rather than that of one or two isolated individuals. One might almost say that Hamsun's vision has become social at last, were it not for his continued accentuation of the irreconcilable conflict between the individual and the group.

"Segelfoss Town" in 1915 and "The Growth of the Soil"—the title ought to be "The Earth's Increase"—in 1918 continue along the path Hamsun entered by "Children of the Time." The scene is laid in his beloved Northland, but the old primitive life is going—going even in the outlying districts, where the pioneers are already breaking ground for new permanent settlements. Business of a modern type has arrived, and much of the quiet humor displayed in these the latest and maturest of Hamsun's works springs from the spectacle of its influence on the natives, whose hands used always to be in their pockets, and whose credulity in face of the improbable was only surpassed by their unwillingness to believe anything reasonable. Still the life he pictures is largely primitive, with nature as man's chief antagonist, and to us of the crowded cities it brings a charm of novelty rarely found in books today. With it goes an understanding of human nature which is no less deep-reaching because it is apt to find expression in whimsical or flagrantly paradoxical forms.

Hamsun has just celebrated his sixtieth birthday anniversary. He is as strong and active as ever, burying himself most of the time on his little estate in the heart of the country that has become to such a peculiar extent his own. There is every reason to expect from him works that may not only equal but surpass the best of his production so far. But even if such expectations should prove false, the body of his work already accomplished is such, both in quantity and quality, that he must perforce be placed in the very front rank of the world's living writers. To the English-speaking world he has so far been made known only through the casual publication at long intervals of a few of his books: "Hunger," "Fictoria" and "Shallow Soil" (rendered in the list above as "New Earth"). There is now reason to believe that this negligence will be remedied, and that soon the best of Hamsun's work will be available in English. To the American and English publics it ought to prove a welcome tonic because of its very divergence from what they commonly feed on. And they may safely look to Hamsun as a thinker as well as a poet and laughing dreamer, provided they realize from the start that his thinking is suggestive rather than conclusive, and that he never meant it to be anything else.

EDWIN BJÖRKMAN.

Part I

It was during the time I wandered about and starved in Christiania: Christiania, this singular city, from which no man departs without carrying away the traces of his sojourn there.

I was lying awake in my attic and I heard a clock below strike six. It was already broad daylight, and people had begun to go up and down the stairs. By the door where the wall of the room was papered with old numbers of the Morgenbladet, I could distinguish clearly a notice from the Director of Lighthouses, and a little to the left of that an inflated advertisement of Fabian Olsens' new-baked bread.

The instant I opened my eyes I began, from sheer force of habit, to think if I had anything to rejoice over that day. I had been somewhat hard-up lately, and one after the other of my belongings had been taken to my "Uncle." I had grown nervous and irritable. A few times I had kept my bed for the day with vertigo. Now and then, when luck had favoured me, I had managed to get five shillings for a feuilleton from some newspaper or other.

It grew lighter and lighter, and I took to reading the advertisements near the door. I could even make out the grinning lean letters of "winding-sheets to be had at Miss Andersen's" on the right of it. That occupied me for a long while. I heard the clock below strike eight as I got up and put on my clothes.

I opened the window and looked out. From where I was standing I had a view of a clothes, line and an open field. Farther away lay the ruins of a burnt-out smithy, which some labourers were busy clearing away. I leant with my elbows resting on the window-frame and gazed into open space. It promised to be a clear day—autumn, that tender, cool time of the year, when all things change their colour, and die, had come to us. The ever-increasing noise in the streets lured me out. The bare room, the floor of which rocked up and down with every step I took across it, seemed like a gasping, sinister coffin. There was no proper fastening to the door, either, and no stove. I used to lie on my socks at night to dry them a little by the morning. The only thing I had to divert myself with was a little red rocking-chair, in which I used to sit in the evenings and doze and muse on all manner of things. When it blew hard, and the door below stood open, all kinds of eerie sounds moaned up through the floor and from out the walls, and the Morgenbladet near the door was rent in strips a span long.

I stood up and searched through a bundle in the corner by the bed for a bite for breakfast, but finding nothing, went back to the window.

God knows, thought I, if looking for employment will ever again avail me aught. The frequent re pulses, half-promises, and curt Noes, the cherished, deluded hopes, and fresh endeavours that always resulted in nothing had done my courage to death. As a last resource, I had applied for a place as debt collector, but I was too late, and, besides, I could not have found the fifty shillings demanded as security. There was always something or another in my way. I had even offered to enlist in the Fire Brigade. There we stood and waited in the vestibule, some half-hundred men, thrusting our chests out to give an idea of strength and bravery, whilst an inspector walked up and down and scanned the applicants, felt their arms, and put one question or another to them. Me, he passed by, merely shaking his head, saying I was rejected on account of my sight. I applied again without my glasses, stood there with knitted brows, and made my eyes as sharp as needles, but the man passed me by again with a smile; he had recognized me. And, worse than all, I could no longer apply for a situation in the garb of a respectable man.

How regularly and steadily things had gone downhill with me for a long time, till, in the end, I was so curiously bared of every conceivable thing. I had not even a comb left, not even a book to read, when things grew all too sad with me. All through the summer, up in the churchyards or parks, where I used to sit and write my articles for the newspapers, I had thought out column after column on the most miscellaneous subjects. Strange ideas, quaint fancies, conceits of my restless brain; in despair I had often chosen the most remote themes, that cost me long hours of intense effort, and never were accepted. When one piece was finished I set to work at another. I was not often discouraged by the editors' "no." I used to tell myself constantly that some day I was bound to succeed; and really occasionally when I was in luck's way, and made a hit with something, I could get five shillings for an afternoon's work.

Once again I raised myself from the window, went over to the washing-stand, and sprinkled some water on the shiny knees of my trousers to dull them a little and make them look a trifle newer. Having done this, I pocketed paper and pencil as usual and went out. I stole very quietly down the stairs in order not to attract my landlady's attention (a few days had elapsed since my rent had fallen due, and I had no longer anything wherewith to raise it).

It was nine o'clock. The roll of vehicles and hum of voices filled the air, a mighty morning-choir mingled with the footsteps of the pedestrians, and the crack of the hack-drivers' whips. The clamorous traffic everywhere exhilarated me at once, and I began to feel more and more contented. Nothing was farther from my intention than to merely take a morning walk in the open air. What had the air to do with my lungs? I was strong as a giant; could stop a dray with my shoulders. A sweet, unwonted mood, a feeling of lightsome happy-go-luckiness took possession of me. I fell to observing the people I met and who passed me, to reading the placards on the wall, noted even the impression of a glance thrown at me from a passing tram-car, let each bagatelle, each trifling incident that crossed or vanished from my path impress me.

If one only had just a little to eat on such a lightsome day! The sense of the glad morning overwhelmed me; my satisfaction became ill-regulated, and for no definite reason I began to hum joyfully.

At a butcher's stall a woman stood speculating on sausage for dinner. As I passed her she looked up at me. She had but one tooth in the front of her head. I had become so nervous and easily affected in the last few days that the woman's face made a loathsome impression upon me. The long yellow snag looked like a little finger pointing out of her gum, and her gaze was still full of sausage as she turned it upon me. I immediately lost all appetite, and a feeling of nausea came over me. When I reached the market-place I went to the fountain and drank a little. I looked up; the dial marked ten on Our Saviour's tower.

I went on through the streets, listlessly, without troubling myself about anything at all, stopped aimlessly at a corner, turned off into a side street without having any errand there. I simply let myself go, wandered about in the pleasant morning, swinging myself care-free to and fro amongst other happy human beings. This air was clear and bright and my mind too was without a shadow.

For quite ten minutes I had had an old lame man ahead of me. He carried a bundle in one hand and exerted his whole body, using all his strength in his endeavours to get along speedily. I could hear how he panted from the exertion, and it occurred to me that I might offer to bear his bundle for him, but yet I made no effort to overtake him. Up in Graendsen I met Hans Pauli, who nodded and hurried past me. Why was he in such a hurry? I had not the slightest intention of asking him for a shilling, and, more than that, I intended at the very first opportunity to return him a blanket which I had borrowed from him some weeks before.

Just wait until I could get my foot on the ladder, I would be beholden to no man, not even for a blanket. Perhaps even this very day I might commence an article on the "Crimes of Futurity," "Freedom of Will," or what not, at any rate, something worth reading, something for which I would at least get ten shillings.... And at the thought of this article I felt myself fired with a desire to set to work immediately and to draw from the contents of my overflowing brain. I would find a suitable place to write in the park and not rest until I had completed my article.

But the old cripple was still making the same sprawling movements ahead of me up the street. The sight of this infirm creature constantly in front of me, commenced to irritate me—his journey seemed endless; perhaps he had made up his mind to go to exactly the same place as I had, and I must needs have him before my eyes the whole way. In my irritation it seemed to me that he slackened his pace a little at every cross street, as if waiting to see which direction I intended to take, upon which he would again swing his bundle in the air and peg away with all his might to keep ahead of me. I follow and watch this tiresome creature and get more and more exasperated with him, I am conscious that he has, little by little, destroyed my happy mood and dragged the pure, beautiful morning down to the level of his own ugliness. He looks like a great sprawling reptile striving with might and main to win a place in the world and reserve the footpath for himself. When we reached the top of the hill I determined to put up with it no longer. I turned to a shop window and stopped in order to give him an opportunity of getting ahead, but when, after a lapse of some minutes, I again walked on there was the man still in front of me—he too had stood stock still,—without stopping to reflect I made three or four furious onward strides, caught him up, and slapped him on the shoulder.

He stopped directly, and we both stared at one another fixedly. "A halfpenny for milk!" he whined, twisting his head askew.

So that was how the wind blew. I felt in my pockets and said: "For milk, eh? Hum-m—money's scarce these times, and I don't really know how much you are in need of it."

"I haven't eaten a morsel since yesterday in Drammen; I haven't got a farthing, nor have I got any work yet!"

"Are you an artisan?"

"Yes; a binder."

"A what?"

"A shoe-binder; for that matter, I can make shoes too."

"Ah, that alters the case," said I, "you wait here for some, minutes and I shall go and get a little money for you; just a few pence."

I hurried as fast as I could down Pyle Street, where I knew of a pawnbroker on a second-floor (one, besides, to whom I had never been before). When I got inside the hall I hastily took off my waistcoat, rolled it up, and put it under my arm; after which I went upstairs and knocked at the office door. I bowed on entering, and threw the waistcoat on the counter.

"One-and-six," said the man.

"Yes, yes, thanks," I replied. "If it weren't that it was beginning to be a little tight for me, of course I wouldn't part with it."

I got the money and the ticket, and went back. Considering all things, pawning that waistcoat was a capital notion. I would have money enough over for a plentiful breakfast, and before evening my thesis on the "Crimes of Futurity" would be ready. I began to find existence more alluring; and I hurried back to the man to get rid of him.

"There it is," said I. "I am glad you applied to me first."

The man took the money and scrutinized me closely. At what was he standing there staring? I had a feeling that he particularly examined the knees of my trousers, and his shameless effrontery bored me. Did the scoundrel imagine that I really was as poor as I looked? Had I not as good as begun to write an article for half-a-sovereign? Besides, I had no fear whatever for the future. I had many irons in the fire. What on earth business was it of an utter stranger if I chose to stand him a drink on such a lovely day? The man's look annoyed me, and I made up my mind to give him a good dressing-down before I left him. I threw back my shoulders, and said:

"My good fellow, you have adopted a most unpleasant habit of staring at a man's knees when he gives you a shilling."

He leant his head back against the wall and opened his mouth widely; something was working in that empty pate of his, and he evidently came to the conclusion that I meant to best him in some way, for he handed me back the money. I stamped on the pavement, and, swearing at him, told him to keep it. Did he imagine I was going to all that trouble for nothing? If all came to all, perhaps I owed him this shilling; I had just recollected an old debt; he was standing before an honest man, honourable to his finger-tips—in short, the money was his. Oh, no thanks were needed; it had been a pleasure to me. Good-bye!

I went on. At last I was freed from this work-ridden plague, and I could go my way in peace. I turned down Pyle Street again, and stopped before a grocer's shop. The whole window was filled with eatables, and I decided to go in and get something to take with me.

"A piece of cheese and a French roll," I said, and threw my sixpence on to the counter.

"Bread and cheese for the whole of it?" asked the woman ironically, without looking up at me.

"For the whole sixpence? Yes," I answered, unruffled.

I took them up, bade the fat old woman good-morning, with the utmost politeness, and sped, full tilt, up Castle Hill to the park.

I found a bench to myself, and began to bite greedily into my provender. It did me good; it was a long time since I had had such a square meal, and, by degrees, I felt the same sated quiet steal over me that one feels after a good long cry. My courage rose mightily. I could no longer be satisfied with writing an article about anything so simple and straight-ahead as the "Crimes of Futurity," that any ass might arrive at, ay, simply deduct from history. I felt capable of a much greater effort than that; I was in a fitting mood to overcome difficulties, and I decided on a treatise, in three sections, on "Philosophical Cognition." This would, naturally, give me an opportunity of crushing pitiably some of Kant's sophistries ... but, on taking out my writing materials to commence work, I discovered that I no longer owned a pencil: I had forgotten it in the pawn-office. My pencil was lying in my waistcoat pocket.

Good Lord! how everything seems to take a delight in thwarting me today! I swore a few times, rose from the seat, and took a couple of turns up and down the path. It was very quiet all around me; down near the Queen's arbour two nursemaids were trundling their perambulators; otherwise, there was not a creature anywhere in sight. I was in a thoroughly embittered temper; I paced up and down before my seat like a maniac. How strangely awry things seemed to go! To think that an article in three sections should be downright stranded by the simple fact of my not having a pennyworth of pencil in my pocket. Supposing I were to return to Pyle Street and ask to get my pencil back? There would be still time to get a good piece finished before the promenading public commenced to fill the parks. So much, too, depended on this treatise on "Philosophical Cognition"—mayhap many human beings' welfare, no one could say; and I told myself it might be of the greatest possible help to many young people. On second thoughts, I would not lay violent hands on Kant; I might easily avoid doing that; I would only need to make an almost imperceptible gliding over when I came to query Time and Space; but I would not answer for Renan, old Parson Renan....

At all events, an article of so-and-so many columns has to be completed. For the unpaid rent, and the landlady's inquiring look in the morning when I met her on the stairs, tormented me the whole day; it rose up and confronted me again and again, even in my pleasant hours, when I had otherwise not a gloomy thought.

I must put an end to it, so I left the park hurriedly to fetch my pencil from the pawnbroker's.

As I arrived at the foot of the hill I overtook two ladies, whom I passed. As I did so, I brushed one of them accidentally on the arm. I looked up; she had a full, rather pale, face. But she blushes, and, becomes suddenly surprisingly lovely. I know not why she blushes; maybe at some word she hears from a passer-by, maybe only at some lurking thought of her own. Or can it be because I touched her arm? Her high, full bosom heaves violently several times, and she closes her hand tightly above the handle of her parasol. What has come to her?

I stopped, and let her pass ahead again. I could, for the moment, go no further; the whole thing struck me as being so singular. I was in a tantalizing mood, annoyed with myself on account of the pencil incident, and in a high degree disturbed by all the food I had taken on a totally empty stomach. Suddenly my thoughts, as if whimsically inspired, take a singular direction. I feel myself seized with an odd desire to make this lady afraid; to follow her, and annoy her in some way. I overtake her again, pass her by, turn quickly round, and meet her face-to-face in order to observe her well. I stand and gaze into her eyes, and hit, on the spur of the moment, on a name which I have never heard before—a name with a gliding, nervous sound—Ylajali! When she is quite close to me I draw myself up and say impressively:

"You are losing your book, madam!" I could hear my heart beat audibly as I said it.

"My book?" she asks her companion, and she walks on.

My devilment waxed apace, and I followed them. At the same time, I was fully conscious that I was playing a mad prank without being able to stop myself. My disordered condition ran away with me; I was inspired with the craziest notions, which I followed blindly as they came to me. I couldn't help it, no matter how much I told myself that I was playing the fool. I made the most idiotic grimaces behind the lady's back, and coughed frantically as I passed her by. Walking on in this manner—very slowly, and always a few steps in advance—I felt her eyes on my back, and involuntarily put down my head with shame for having caused her annoyance. By degrees, a wonderful feeling stole over me of being far, far away in other places; I had a half-undefined sense that it was not I who was going along over the gravel hanging my head.

A few minutes later, they reached Pascha's bookshop. I had already stopped at the first window, and as they go by I step forward and repeat:

"You are losing your book, madam!"

"No; what book?" she asks affrightedly. "Can you make out what book it is he is talking about?" and she comes to a stop.

I hug myself with delight at her confusion; the irresolute perplexity in her eyes positively fascinates me. Her mind cannot grasp my short, passionate address. She has no book with her; not a single page of a book, and yet she fumbles in her pockets, looks down repeatedly at her hands, turns her head and scrutinizes the streets behind her, exerts her sensitive little brain to the utmost in trying to discover what book it is I am talking about. Her face changes colour, has now one, now another expression, and she is breathing quite audibly—even the very buttons on her gown seem to stare at me, like a row of frightened eyes.

"Don't bother about him!" says her companion, taking her by the arm. "He is drunk; can't you see that the man is drunk?"

Strange as I was at this instant to myself, so absolutely a prey to peculiar invisible inner influences, nothing occurred around me without my observing it. A large, brown dog sprang right across the street towards the shrubbery, and then down towards the Tivoli; he had on a very narrow collar of German silver. Farther up the street a window opened on the second floor, and a servant-maid leant out of it, with her sleeves turned up, and began to clean the panes on the outside. Nothing escaped my notice; I was clear-headed and ready-witted. Everything rushed in upon me with a gleaming distinctness, as if I were suddenly surrounded by a strong light. The ladies before me had each a blue bird's wing in their hats, and a plaid silk ribbon round their necks. It struck me that they were sisters.

They turned, stopped at Cisler's music-shop, and spoke together. I stopped also. Thereupon they both came back, went the same road as they had come, passed me again, and turned the corner of University Street and up towards St. Olav's place. I was all the time as close at their heels as I dared to be. They turned round once, and sent me a half-fearful, half-questioning look, and I saw no resentment nor any trace of a frown in it.

This forbearance with my annoyance shamed me thoroughly and made me lower my eyes. I would no longer be a trouble to them; out of sheer gratitude I would follow them with my gaze, not lose sight of them until they entered some place safely and disappeared.

Outside No. 2, a large four-storied house, they turned again before going in. I leant against a lamp-post near the fountain and listened for their footsteps on the stairs. They died away on the second floor. I advanced from the lamp-post and looked up at the house. Then something odd happened. The curtains above were stirred, and a second after a window opened, a head popped out, and two singular-looking eyes dwelt on me. "Ylajali!" I muttered, half-aloud, and I felt I grew red.

Why does she not call for help, or push over one of these flower-pots and strike me on the head, or send some one down to drive me away? We stand and look into one another's eyes without moving; it lasts a minute. Thoughts dart between the window and the street, and not a word is spoken. She turns round, I feel a wrench in me, a delicate shock through my senses; I see a shoulder that turns, a back that disappears across the floor. That reluctant turning from the window, the accentuation in that movement of the shoulders was like a nod to me. My blood was sensible of all the delicate, dainty greeting, and I felt all at once rarely glad. Then I wheeled round and went down the street.

I dared not look back, and knew not if she had returned to the window. The more I considered this question the more nervous and restless I became. Probably at this very moment she was standing watching closely all my movements. It is by no means comfortable to know that you are being watched from behind your back. I pulled myself together as well as I could and proceeded on my way; my legs began to jerk under me, my gait became unsteady just because I purposely tried to make it look well. In order to appear at ease and

trying to look normal made him look less at ease

indifferent, I flung my arms about, spat out, and threw my head well back—all without avail, for I continually felt the pursuing eyes on my neck, and a cold shiver ran down my back. At length I escaped down a side street, from which I took the road to Pyle Street to get my pencil.

I had no difficulty in recovering it; the man brought me the waistcoat himself, and as he did so, begged me to search through all the pockets. I found also a couple of pawn-tickets which I pocketed as I thanked the obliging little man for his civility. I was more and more taken with him, and grew all of a sudden extremely anxious to make a favourable impression on this person. I took a turn towards the door and then back again to the counter as if I had forgotten something. It struck me that I owed him an explanation, that I ought to elucidate matters a little. I began to hum in order to attract his attention. Then, taking the pencil in my hand, I held it up and said:

"It would never have entered my head to come such a long way for any and every bit of pencil, but with this one it was quite a different matter; there Was another reason, a special reason. Insignificant as it looked, this stump of pencil had simply made me what I was in the world, so to say, placed me in life." I said no more. The man had come right over to the counter.

"Indeed!" said he, and he looked inquiringly at me.

"It was with this pencil," I continued, in cold blood, "that I wrote my dissertation on 'Philosophical Cognition,' in three volumes." Had he never heard mention of it?

Well, he did seem to remember having heard the name, rather the title.

"Yes," said I, "that was by me, so it was." So he must really not be astonished that I should be desirous of having the little bit of pencil back again. I valued it far too highly to lose it; why, it was almost as much to me as a little human creature. For the rest I was honestly grateful to him for his civility, and I would bear him in mind for it. Yes, truly, I really would. A promise was a promise; that was the sort of man I was, and he really deserved it. "Good-bye!" I walked to the door with the bearing of one who had it in his power to place a man in a high position, say in the fire-office. The honest pawnbroker bowed twice profoundly to me as I withdrew. I turned again and repeated my good-bye.

On the stairs I met a woman with a travelling-bag in her hand, who squeezed diffidently against the wall to make room for me, and I voluntarily thrust my hand in my pocket for something to give her, and looked foolish as I found nothing and passed on with my head down. I heard her knock at the office door; there was an alarm over it, and I recognized the jingling sound it gave when any one rapped on the door with his knuckles.

The sun stood in the south; it was about twelve. The whole town began to get on its legs as it approached the fashionable hour for promenading. Bowing and laughing folk walked up and down Carl Johann Street. I stuck my elbows closely to my sides, tried to make myself look small, and slipped unperceived past some acquaintances who had taken up their stand at the corner of University Street to gaze at the passers-by. I wandered up Castle Hill and fell into a reverie.

How gaily and lightly these people I met carried their radiant heads, and swung themselves through life as through a ball-room! There was no sorrow in a single look I met, no burden on any shoulder, perhaps not even a clouded thought, not a little hidden pain in any of the happy souls. And I, walking in the very midst of these people, young and newly-fledged as I was, had already forgotten the very look of happiness. I hugged these thoughts to myself as I went on, and found that a great injustice had been done me. Why had the last months pressed so strangely hard on me? I failed to recognize my own happy temperament, and I met with the most singular annoyances from all quarters. I could not sit down on a bench by myself or set my foot any place without being assailed by insignificant accidents, miserable details, that forced their way into my imagination and scattered my powers to all the four winds. A dog that dashed by me, a yellow rose in a man's buttonhole, had the power to set my thoughts vibrating and occupy me for a length of time.

What was it that ailed me? Was the hand of the Lord turned against me? But why just against me? Why, for that matter, not just as well against a man in South America? When I considered the matter over, it grew more and more incomprehensible to me that I of all others should be selected as an experiment for a Creator's whims. It was, to say the least of it, a peculiar mode of procedure to pass over a whole world of other humans in order to reach me. Why not select just as well Bookseller Pascha, or Hennechen the steam agent?

As I went my way I sifted this thing, and could not get quit of it. I found the most weighty arguments against the Creator's arbitrariness in letting me pay for all the others' sins. Even after I had found a seat and sat down, the query persisted in occupying me, and prevented me from thinking of aught else. From the day in May when my ill-luck began I could so clearly notice my gradually increasing debility; I had become, as it were, too languid to control or lead myself whither I would go. A swarm of tiny noxious animals had bored a way into my inner man and hollowed me out.

Supposing God Almighty simply intended to annihilate me? I got up and paced backwards and forwards before the seat.

My whole being was at this moment in the highest degree of torture, I had pains in my arms, and could hardly bear to hold them in the usual way. I experienced also great discomfort from my last full meal; I was oversated, and walked backwards and forwards without looking up. The people who came and went around me glided past me like faint gleams. At last my seat was taken up by two men, who lit cigars and began to talk loudly together. I got angry and was on the point of addressing them, but turned on my heel and went right to the other end of the Park, and found another seat. I sat down.

The thought of God began to occupy me. It seemed to me in the highest degree indefensible of Him to interfere every time I sought for a place, and to upset the whole thing, while all the time I was but imploring enough for a daily meal.

I had remarked so plainly that, whenever I had been hungry for any length of time, it was just as if my brains ran quite gently out of my head and left me with a vacuum—my head grew light and far off, I no longer felt its weight on my shoulders, and I had a consciousness that my eyes stared far too widely open when I looked at anything.

I sat there on the seat and pondered over all this, and grew more and more bitter against God for His prolonged inflictions. If He meant to draw me nearer to Him, and make me better by exhausting me and placing obstacle after obstacle in my way, I could assure Him He made a slight mistake. And, almost crying with defiance, I looked up towards Heaven and told Him so mentally, once and for all.

Fragments of the teachings of my childhood ran through my memory. The rhythmical sound of Biblical language sang in my ears, and I talked quite softly to myself, and held my head sneeringly askew. Wherefore should I sorrow for what I eat, for what I drink, or for what I may array this miserable food for worms called my earthy body? Hath not my Heavenly Father provided for me, even as for the sparrow on the housetop, and hath He not in His graciousness pointed towards His lowly servitor? The Lord stuck His finger in the net of my nerves gently—yea, verily, in desultory fashion—and brought slight disorder among the threads. And then the Lord withdrew His finger, and there were fibres and delicate root-like filaments adhering to the finger, and they were the nerve-threads of the filaments. And there was a gaping hole after the finger, which was God's finger, and a wound in my brain in the track of His finger. But when God had touched me with His finger, He let me be, and touched me no more, and let no evil befall me; but let me depart in peace, and let me depart with the gaping hole. And no evil hath befallen me from the God who is the Lord God of all Eternity.

The sound of music was borne up on the wind to me from the Students' Allée. It was therefore past two o'clock. I took out my writing materials to try to write something, and at the same time my book of shaving-tickets[1] fell out of my pocket. I opened it, and counted the tickets; there were six. "The Lord be praised," I exclaimed involuntarily; "I can still get shaved for a couple of weeks, and look a little decent"; and I immediately fell into a better frame of mind on account of this little property which still remained to me. I smoothed the leaves out carefully, and put the book safely into my pocket.

But write I could not. After a few lines nothing seemed to occur to me; my thought ran in other directions, and I could not pull myself together enough for any special exertion.

Everything influenced and distracted me; everything I saw made a fresh impression on me. Flies and tiny mosquitoes stick fast to the paper and disturb me. I blow at them to get rid of them—blow harder and harder; to no purpose, the little pests throw themselves on their backs, make themselves heavy, and fight against me until their slender legs bend. They are not to be moved from the spot; they find something to hook on to, set their heels against a comma or an unevenness in the paper, or stand immovably still until they themselves think fit to go their way.

These insects continued to busy me for a long time, and I crossed my legs to observe them at leisure. All at once a couple of high clarionet notes waved up to me from the bandstand, and gave my thoughts a new impulse.

Despondent at not being able to put my article together, I replaced the paper in my pocket, and leant back in the seat. At this instant my head is so clear that I can follow the most delicate train of thought without tiring. As I lie in this position, and let my eyes glide down my breast and along my legs, I notice the jerking movement my foot makes each time my pulse beats. I half rise and look down at my feet, and I experience at this moment a fantastic and singular feeling that I have never felt before—a delicate, wonderful shock through my nerves, as if sparks of cold light quivered through them—it was as if catching sight of my shoes I had met with a kind old acquaintance, or got back a part of myself that had been riven loose. A feeling of recognition trembles through my senses; the tears well up in my eyes, and I have a feeling as if my shoes are a soft, murmuring strain rising towards me. "Weakness!" I cried harshly to myself, and I clenched my fists and I repeated "Weakness!" I laughed at myself, for this ridiculous feeling, made fun of myself, with a perfect consciousness of doing so, talked very severely and sensibly, and closed my eyes very tightly to get rid of the tears.

As if I had never seen my shoes before, I set myself to study their looks, their characteristics, and, when I stir my foot, their shape and their worn uppers. I discover that their creases and white seams give

---

[1] Issued by the barbers at cheaper rates, as few men in Norway shave themselves.

them expression—impart a physiognomy to them. Something of my own nature had gone over into these shoes; they affected me, like a ghost of my other I— a breathing portion of my very self.

I sat and toyed with these fancies a long time, perhaps an entire hour. A little, old man came and took the other end of the seat; as he seated himself he panted after his walk, and muttered:

"Ay, ay, ay, ay, ay, ay, ay, ay, ay, ay; very true!"

As soon as I heard his voice, I felt as if a wind had swept through my head. I let shoes be shoes, and it seemed to me that the distracted phase of mind I had just experienced dated from a long-vanished period, maybe a year or two back, and was about to be quietly effaced from my memory. I began to observe the old fellow.

Did this little man concern me in any way? Not in the least, not in the very slightest degree! Only that he held a newspaper in his hand, an old number (with the advertisement sheet on the outside), in which something or other seemed to be rolled up; my curiosity was aroused, and I could not take my eyes away from this paper. The insane idea entered my head that it might be a quite peculiar newspaper—unique of its kind. My curiosity increased, and I began to move backwards and forwards on the seat. It might contain deeds, dangerous documents stolen from some archive or other; something floated before me about a secret treaty—a conspiracy.

The man sat quietly, and pondered. Why did he not carry his newspaper as every other person carries a paper, with its name out? What species of cunning lurked under that? He did not seem either to like letting his package out of his hands, not for anything in the world; perhaps he did not even dare trust it into his own pocket. I could stake my life there was something at the bottom of that package—I considered a bit. Just the fact of finding it so impossible to penetrate this mysterious affair distracted me with curiosity. I searched my pockets for something to offer the man in order to enter into conversation with him, took hold of my shaving-book, but put it back again. Suddenly it entered my head to be utterly audacious; I slapped my empty breast-pocket, and said:

"May I offer you a cigarette?"

"Thank you!" The man did not smoke; he had to give it up to spare his eyes; he was nearly blind. Thank you very much all the same. Was it long since his eyes got bad? In that case, perhaps, he could not read either, not even a paper?

No, not even the newspaper, more's the pity. The man looked at me; his weak eyes were each covered with a film which gave them a glassy appearance; his gaze grew bleary, and made a disgusting impression on me.

"You are a stranger here?" he said.

"Yes." Could he not even read the name of the paper he held in his hand?

"Barely." For that matter, he could hear directly that I was a stranger. There was something in my accent which told him. It did not need much; he could hear so well. At night, when every one slept, he could hear people in the next room breathing....

"What I was going to say was, 'where do you live?'"

On the spur of the moment a lie stood, ready-made, in my head. I lied involuntarily, without any object, without any arrière-pensée, and I answered—

"St. Olav's Place, No. 2."

"Really?" He knew every stone in St. Olav's Place. There was a fountain, some lamp-posts, a few trees; he remembered all of it. "What number do you live in?"

Desirous to put an end to this, I got up. But my notion about the newspaper had driven me to my wit's end; I resolved to clear the thing up, at no matter what cost.

"When you cannot read the paper, why—"

"In No. 2, I think you said," continued the man, without noticing my disturbance. "There was a time I knew every person in No. 2; what is your landlord's name?"

I quickly found a name to get rid of him; invented one on the spur of the moment, and blurted it out to stop my tormentor.

"Happolati!" said I.

"Happolati, ay!" nodded the man; and he never missed a syllable of this difficult name.

I looked at him with amazement; there he sat, gravely, with a considering air. Before I had well given utterance to the stupid name which jumped into my head the man had accommodated himself to it, and pretended to have heard it before.

In the meantime, he had laid his package on the seat, and I felt my curiosity quiver through my nerves. I noticed there were a few grease spots on the paper.

"Isn't he a sea-faring man, your landlord?" queried he, and there was not a trace of suppressed irony in his voice; "I seem to remember he was."

"Sea-faring man? Excuse me, it must be the brother you know; this man is namely J. A. Happolati, the agent."

I thought this would finish him; but he willingly fell in with everything I said. If I had found a name like Barrabas Rosebud it would not have roused his suspicions.

"He is an able man, I have heard?" he said, feeling his way.

"Oh, a clever fellow!" answered I; "a thorough business head; agent for every possible thing going. Cranberries from China; feathers and down from Russia; hides, pulp, writing-ink—"

"He, he! the devil he is?" interrupted the old chap, highly excited.

This began to get interesting. The situation ran away with me, and one lie after another engendered in my head. I sat down again, forgot the newspaper, and the remarkable documents, grew lively, and cut short the old fellow's talk.

The little goblin's unsuspecting simplicity made me foolhardy; I would stuff him recklessly full of lies; rout him out o' field grandly, and stop his mouth from sheer amazement.

Had he heard of the electric psalm-book that Happolati had invented?

"What? Elec—"

"With electric letters that could give light in the dark! a perfectly extraordinary enterprise. A million crowns to be put in circulation; foundries and printing-presses at work, and shoals of regular mechanics to be employed; I had heard as many as seven hundred men."

"Ay, isn't it just what I say?" drawled out the man calmly.

He said no more, he believed every word I related, and for all that, he was not taken aback. This disappointed me a little; I had expected to see him utterly bewildered by my inventions.

I searched my brain for a couple of desperate lies, went the whole hog, hinted that Happolati had been Minister of State for nine years in Persia. "You perhaps have no conception of what it means to be Minister of State in Persia?" I asked. It was more than king here, or about the same as Sultan, if he knew what that meant, but Happolati had managed the whole thing, and was never at a loss. And I related about his daughter Ylajali, a fairy, a princess, who had three hundred slaves, and who reclined on a couch of yellow roses. She was the loveliest creature I had ever seen; I had, may the Lord strike me, never seen her match for looks in my life!

"So—o; was she so lovely?" remarked the old fellow, with an absent air, as he gazed at the ground.

"Lovely? She was beauteous, she was sinfully fascinating. Eyes like raw silk, arms of amber! Just one glance from her was as seductive as a kiss; and when she called me, her voice darted like a wine-ray right into my soul's phosphor. And why shouldn't she be so beautiful?" Did he imagine she was a messenger or something in the fire brigade? She was simply a Heaven's wonder, I could just inform him, a fairy tale.

"Yes, to be sure!" said he, not a little bewildered. His quiet bored me; I was excited by the sound of my own voice and spoke in utter seriousness; the stolen archives, treaties with some foreign power or other, no longer occupied my thoughts; the little flat bundle of paper lay on the seat between us, and I had no longer the smallest desire to examine it or see what it contained. I was entirely absorbed in stories of my own which floated in singular visions across my mental eye. The blood flew to my head, and I roared with laughter.

At this moment the little man seemed about to go. He stretched himself, and in order not to break off too abruptly, added: "He is said to own much property, this Happolati?"

How dared this bleary-eyed, disgusting old man toss about the rare name I had invented as if it were a common name stuck up over every huckster-shop in the town? He never stumbled over a letter or forgot a syllable. The name had bitten fast in his brain and struck root on the instant. I got annoyed; an inward exasperation surged up in me against this creature whom nothing had the power to disturb and nothing render suspicious.

I therefore replied shortly, "I know nothing about that! I know absolutely nothing whatever about that! Let me inform you once for all that his name is Johann Arendt Happolati, if you go by his own initials."

"Johannn Arendt Happolati!" repeated the man, a little astonished at my vehemence; and with that he grew silent.

"You should see his wife!" I said, beside myself. "A fatter creature ... Eh? what? Perhaps you don't even believe she is really fat?"

Well, indeed he did not see his way to deny that such a man might perhaps have a rather stout wife. The old fellow answered quite gently and meekly to each of my assertions, and sought for words as if he feared to offend and perhaps make me furious.

"Hell and fire, man! Do you imagine that I am sitting here stuffing you chock-full of lies?" I roared furiously. "Perhaps you don't even believe that a man of the name of Happolati exists! I never saw your match for obstinacy and malice in any old man. What the devil ails you? Perhaps, too, into the bargain, you have been all this while thinking to yourself I am a poverty-stricken fellow, sitting here in my Sunday-best without even a case full of cigarettes in my pocket. Let me tell you such treatment as yours is a thing I am not accustomed to, and I won't endure it, the Lord strike me dead if I will—neither from you nor any one else, do you know that?"

The man had risen with his mouth agape; he stood tongue-tied and listened to my outbreak until the end. Then he snatched his parcel from off the seat and went, ay, nearly ran, down the patch, with the short, tottering steps of an old man.

I leant back and looked at the retreating figure that seemed to shrink at each step as it passed away. I do not know from where the impression came, but it appeared to me that I had never in my life seen a more vile back than this one, and I did not regret that I had abused the creature before he left me.

The day began to decline, the sun sank, it commenced to rustle lightly in the trees around, and the nursemaids who sat in groups near the parallel bars made ready to wheel their perambulators home. I was calmed and in good spirit. The excitement I had just laboured under quieted down little by little, and I grew weaker, more languid, and began to feel drowsy. Neither did the quantity of bread I had eaten cause me any longer any particular distress. I leant against the back of the seat in the best of humours, closed my eyes, and got more and more sleepy. I dozed, and was just on the point of falling asleep, when a park-keeper put his hand on my shoulder and said:

"You must not sit here and go to sleep!"

"No?" I said, and sprang immediately up, my unfortunate position rising all at once vividly before my eyes. I must do something; find some way or another out of it. To look for situations had been of no avail to me. Even the recommendations I showed had grown a little old, and were written by people all too little known to be of much use; besides that, constant refusals all through the summer had somewhat disheartened me. At all events, my rent was due, and I must raise the wind for that; the rest would have to wait a little.

Quite involuntarily I had got paper and pencil into my hand again, and I sat and wrote mechanically the date, 1848, in each corner. If only now one single effervescing thought would grip me powerfully, and put words into my mouth. Why, I had known hours when I could write a long piece, without the least exertion, and turn it off capitally, too.

I am sitting on the seat, and I write, scores of times, 1848. I write this date criss-cross, in all possible fashions, and wait until a workable idea shall occur to me. A swarm of loose thoughts flutter about in my head. The feeling of declining day makes me downcast, sentimental; autumn is here, and has already begun to hush everything into sleep and torpor. The flies and insects have received their first warning. Up in the trees and down in the fields the sounds of struggling life can be heard rustling, murmuring, restless; labouring not to perish. The down-trodden existence of the whole insect world is astir for yet a little while. They poke their yellow heads up from the turf, lift their legs, feel their way with long feelers and then collapse suddenly, roll over, and turn their bellies in the air.

Every growing thing has received its peculiar impress: the delicately blown breath of the first cold. The stubbles straggle wanly sunwards, and the falling leaves rustle to the earth, with a sound as of errant silkworms.

It is the reign of Autumn, the height of the Carnival of Decay, the roses have got inflammation in their blushes, an uncanny hectic tinge, through their soft damask.

I felt myself like a creeping thing on the verge of destruction, gripped by ruin in the midst of a whole world ready for lethargic sleep. I rose, oppressed by weird terrors, and took some furious strides down the path. "No!" I cried out, clutching both my hands; "there must be an end to this," and I reseated myself, grasped the pencil, and set seriously to work at an article.

There was no possible use in giving way, with the unpaid rent staring me straight in the face.

Slowly, quite slowly, my thoughts collected. I paid attention to them, and wrote quietly and well; wrote a couple of pages as an introduction. It would serve as a beginning to anything. A description of travel, a political leader, just as I thought fit—it was a perfectly splendid commencement for something or anything. So I took to seeking for some particular subject to handle, a person or a thing, that I might grapple with, and I could find nothing. Along with this fruitless exertion, disorder began to hold its sway again in my thoughts. I felt how my brain positively snapped and my head emptied, until it sat at last, light, buoyant, and void on my shoulders. I was conscious of the gaping vacuum in my skull with every fibre of my being. I seemed to myself to be hollowed out from top and toe.

In my pain I cried: "Lord, my God and Father!" and repeated this cry many times at a stretch, without adding one word more.

The wind soughed through the trees; a storm was brewing. I sat a while longer, and gazed at my paper, lost in thought, then folded it up and put it slowly into my pocket. It got chilly; and I no longer owned a waistcoat. I buttoned my coat right up to my throat and thrust my hands in my pockets; thereupon I rose and went on.

If I had only succeeded this time, just this once. Twice my landlady had asked me with her eyes for payment, and I was obliged to hang my head and slink past her with a shamefaced air. I could not do it again: the very next time I met those eyes I would give warning and account for myself honestly. Well, any way, things could not last long at this rate.

On coming to the exit of the park I saw the old chap I had put to flight. The mysterious new paper parcel lay opened on the seat next him, filled with different sorts of victuals, of which he ate as he sat. I immediately wanted to go over and ask pardon for my conduct, but the sight of food repelled me. The decrepit fingers looked like ten claws as they clutched loathsomely at the greasy bread and butter; I felt qualmish, and passed by without addressing him. He did not recognize me; his eyes stared at me, dry as horn, and his face did not move a muscle.

And so I went on my way.

As customary, I halted before every newspaper placard I came to, to read the announcements of situations vacant, and was lucky enough to find one that I might try for.

A grocer in Groenlandsleret wanted a man every week for a couple of hours' book-keeping; remuneration according to agreement. I noted my man's address, and prayed to God in silence for this place. I would demand less than any one else for my work; sixpence was ample, or perhaps fivepence. That would not matter in the least.

On going home, a slip of paper from my landlady lay on my table, in which she begged me to pay my rent in advance, or else move as soon as I could. I must not be offended, it was absolutely a necessary request. Friendlily Mrs. Gundersen.

I wrote an application to Christy the grocer, No. 13 Groenlandsleret, put it in an envelope, and took it to the pillar at the corner. Then I returned to my room and sat down in the rocking-chair to think, whilst the darkness grew closer and closer. Sitting up late began to be difficult now.

I woke very early in the morning. It was still quite dark as I opened my eyes, and it was not till long after that I heard five strokes of the clock down-stairs. I turned round to doze again, but sleep had down. I grew more and more wakeful, and lay and thought of a thousand things.

Suddenly a few good sentences fitted for a sketch or story strike me, delicate linguistic hits of which I have never before found the equal. I lie and repeat these words over to myself, and find that they are capital. Little by little others come and fit themselves to the preceding ones. I grow keenly wakeful. I get up and snatch paper and pencil from the table behind my bed. It was as if a vein had burst in me; one word follows another, and they fit themselves together harmoniously with telling effect. Scene piles on scene, actions and speeches bubble up in my brain, and a wonderful sense of pleasure empowers me. I write as one possessed, and fill page after page, without a moment's pause.

Thoughts come so swiftly to me and continue to flow so richly that I miss a number of telling bits, that I cannot set down quickly enough, although I work with all my might. They continue to invade me; I am full of my subject, and every word I write is inspired.

This strange period lasts—lasts such a blessedly long time before it comes to an end. I have fifteen—twenty written pages lying on my knees before me, when at last I cease and lay my pencil aside, So sure as there is any worth in these pages, so sure am I saved. I jump out of bed and dress myself, It grows lighter. I can half distinguish the lighthouse director's announcement down near the door, and near the window it is already so light that I could, in case of necessity, see to write. I set to work immediately to make a fair copy of what I have written.

An intense, peculiar exhalation of light and colour emanates from these fantasies of mine. I start with surprise as I note one good thing after another, and tell myself that this is the best thing I have ever read. My head swims with a sense of satisfaction; delight inflates me; I grow grandiose.

I weigh my writing in my hand, and value it, at a loose guess, for five shillings on the spot.

It could never enter any one's head to chaffer about five shillings; on the contrary, getting it for half-a-sovereign might be considered dirt-cheap, considering the quality of the thing.

I had no intention of turning off such special work gratis. As far as I was aware, one did not pick up stories of that kind on the wayside, and I decided on half-a-sovereign.

The room brightened and brightened. I threw a glance towards the door, and could distinguish without particular trouble the skeleton-like letters of Miss Andersen's winding-sheet advertisement to the right of it. It was also a good while since the clock has struck seven.

I rose and came to a standstill in the middle of the floor. Everything well considered, Mrs. Gundersen's warning came rather opportunely. This was, properly speaking, no fit room for me: there were only common enough green curtains at the windows, and neither were there any pegs too many on the wall. The poor little rocking-chair over in the corner was in reality a mere attempt at a rocking-chair; with the smallest sense of humour, one might easily split one's sides with laughter at it. It was far too low for a grown man, and besides that, one needed, so to speak, the aid of a boot-jack to get out of it. To cut it short, the room was not adopted for the pursuit of things intellectual, and I did not intend to keep it any longer. On no account would I keep it. I had held my peace, and endured and lived far too long in such a den.

Buoyed up by hope and satisfaction, constantly occupied with my remarkable sketch, which I drew forth every moment from my pocket and re-read, I determined to set seriously to work with my flitting. I took out my bundle, a red handkerchief that contained a few clean collars and some crumpled newspapers, in which I had occasionally carried home bread. I rolled my blanket up and pocketed my reserve white writing-paper. Then I ransacked every corner to assure myself that I had left nothing behind, and as I could not find anything, went over to the window and looked out.

The morning was gloomy and wet; there was no one about at the burnt-out smithy, and the clothesline down in the yard stretched tightly from wall to wall shrunken by the wet. It was all familiar to me, so I stepped back from the window, took the blanket under my arm, and made a low bow to the lighthouse director's announcement, bowed again to Miss Andersen's winding-sheet advertisement, and opened the door. Suddenly the thought of my land-lady struck me; she really ought to be informed of my leaving, so that she could see she had had an honest soul to deal with.

I wanted also to thank her in writing for the few days' overtime in which I occupied the room. The certainty that I was now saved for some time to come increased so strongly in me that I even promised her five shillings. I would call in some day when passing by.

Besides that, I wanted to prove to her what an upright sort of person her roof had sheltered.

I left the note behind me on the table.

Once again I stopped at the door and turned round; the buoyant feeling of having risen once again to the surface charmed me, and made me feel grateful towards God and all creation, and I knelt down at the bedside and thanked God aloud for His great goodness to me that morning.

I knew it; ah! I knew that the rapture of inspiration I had just felt and noted down was a miraculous heaven-brew in my spirit in answer to my yesterday's cry for aid.

"It was God! It was God!" I cried to myself, and I wept for enthusiasm over my own words; now and then I had to stop and listen if any one was on the stairs. At last I rose up and prepared to go. I stole noiselessly down each flight and reached the door unseen.

The streets were glistening from the rain which had fallen in the early morning. The sky hung damp and heavy over the town, and there was no glint of sunlight visible. I wondered what the day would bring forth? I went as usual in the direction of the Town Hall, and saw that it was half-past eight. I had yet a few hours to walk about; there was no use in going to the newspaper office before ten, perhaps eleven. I must lounge about so long, and think, in the meantime, over some expedient to raise breakfast. For that matter, I had no fear of going to bed hungry that day; those times were over, God be praised! That was a thing of the past, an evil dream. Henceforth, Excelsior!

But, in the meanwhile, the green blanket was a trouble to me. Neither could I well make myself conspicuous by carrying such a thing about right under people's eyes. What would any one think of me? And as I went on I tried to think of a place where I could have it kept till later on. It occurred to me that I might go into Semb's and get it wrapped up in paper; not only would it look better, but I need no longer be ashamed of carrying it,

I entered the shop, and stated my errand to one of the shop boys.

He looked first at the blanket, then at me. It struck me that he shrugged his shoulders to himself a little contemptuously as he took it; this annoyed me.

"Young man," I cried, "do be a little careful! There are two costly glass vases in that; the parcel has to go to Smyrna."

This had a famous effect. The fellow apologized with every movement he made for not having guessed that there was something out of the common in this blanket. When he had finished packing it up I thanked him with the air of a man who had sent precious goods to Smyrna before now. He held the door open for me, and bowed twice as I left.

I began to wander about amongst the people in the market place, kept from choice near the woman who had potted plants for sale. The heavy crimson roses—the leaves of which glowed blood-like and moist in the damp morning—made me envious, and tempted me sinfully to snatch one, and I inquired the price of them merely as an excuse to approach as near to them as possible.

If I had any money over I would buy one, no matter how things went; indeed, I might well save a little now and then out of my way of living to balance things again.

It was ten o'clock, and I went up to the newspaper office. "Scissors" is running through a lot of old papers. The editor has not come yet. On being asked my business, I delivered my weighty manuscript, lead him to suppose that it is something of more than uncommon importance, and impress upon his memory gravely that he is to give it into we editor's own hands as soon as he arrives.

I would myself call later on in the day for an answer.

"All right," replied "Scissors," and busied himself again with his papers.

It seemed to me that he treated the matter somewhat too coolly; but I said nothing, only nodded rather carelessly to him, and left.

I had now time on hand! If it would only clear up! It was perfectly wretched weather, without either wind or freshness. Ladies carried their umbrellas, to be on the safe side, and the woollen caps of the men looked limp and depressing.

I took another turn across the market and looked at the vegetables and roses. I feel a hand on my shoulder and turn round—"Missy" bids me good morning! "Good-morning!" I say in return, a little questioningly. I never cared particularly for "Missy."

He looks inquisitively at the large brand-new parcel under my arm, and asks:

"What have you got there?"

"Oh, I have been down to Semb and got some cloth for a suit," I reply, in a careless tone. "I didn't think I could rub on any longer; there's such a thing as treating oneself too shabbily."

He looks at me with an amazed start.

"By the way, how are you getting on?" He asks it slowly.

"Oh, beyond all expectation!"

"Then you have got something to do now?"

"Something to do?" I answer and seem surprised. "Rather! Why, I am book-keeper at Christensen's—a wholesale house."

"Oh, indeed!" he remarks and draws back a little.

"Well, God knows I am the first to be pleased at your success. If only you don't let people beg the money from you that you earn. Good-day!"

A second after he wheels round and comes back and, pointing with his cane to my parcel, says:

"I would recommend my tailor to you for the suit of clothes. You won't find a better tailor than Isaksen—just say I sent you, that's all!"

This was really rather more than I could swallow. What did he want to poke his nose in my affairs for? Was it any concern of his which tailor I employed? The sight of this empty-headed dandified "masher" embittered me, and I reminded him rather brutally of ten shilling he had borrowed from me. But before he could reply I regretted that I had asked for it. I got ashamed and avoided meeting his eyes, and, as a lady came by just then, I stepped hastily aside to let her pass, and seized the opportunity to proceed on my way.

What should I do with myself whilst I waited? I could not visit a cafe with empty pockets, and I knew of no acquaintance that I could call on at this time of day. I wended my way instinctively up town, killed a good deal of time between the marketplace and the Graendsen, read Aftenposten, which was newly posted up on the board outside the office, took a turn down Carl Johann, wheeled round and went straight on to Our Saviour's Cemetery, where I found a quiet seat on the slope near the Mortuary Chapel.

I sat there in complete quietness, dozed in the damp air, mused, half-slept and shivered.

And time passed. Now, was it certain that the story really was a little masterpiece of inspired art? God knows if it might not have its faults here and there. All things well weighed, it was not certain that it would be accepted; no, simply not even accepted. It was perhaps mediocre enough in its way, perhaps downright worthless. What security had I that it was not already at this moment lying in the waste-paper basket?... My confidence was shaken. I sprang up and stormed out of the graveyard.

Down in Akersgaden I peeped into a shop window, and saw that it was only a little past noon. There was no use in looking up the editor before four. The fate of my story filled me with gloomy forebodings; the more I thought about it the more absurd it seemed to me that I could have written anything useable with such suddenness, half-asleep, with my brain full of fever and dreams. Of course I had deceived myself and been happy all through the long morning for nothing!... Of course!... I rushed with hurried strides up Ullavold-sveien, past St. Han's Hill, until I came to the open fields; on through the narrow quaint lanes in Sagene, past waste plots and small tilled fields, and found myself at last on a country road, the end of which I could not see.

Here I halted and decided to turn.

I was warm from the walk, and returned slowly and very downcast. I met two hay-carts. The drivers were lying flat upon the top of their loads, and sang. Both were bare-headed, and both had round, care-free faces. I passed them and thought to myself that they were sure to accost me, sure to fling some taunt or other at me, play me some trick; and as I got near enough, one of them called out and asked what I had under my arm?

"A blanket!"

"What o'clock is it?" he asked then.

"I don't know rightly; about three, I think!" Whereupon they both laughed and drove on. I felt at the same moment the lash of a whip curl round one of my ears, and my hat was jerked off. They couldn't let me pass without playing me a trick. I raised my hand to my head more or less confusedly, picked my hat out of the ditch, and continued on my way. Down at St. Han's Hill I met a man who told me it was past four. Past four! already past four! I mended my pace, nearly ran down to the town, turned off towards the news office. Perhaps the editor had been there hours ago, and had left the office by now. I ran, jostled against folk, stumbled, knocked against cars, left everybody behind me, competed with the very horses, struggled like a madman to arrive there in time. I wrenched through the door, took the stairs in four bounds, and knocked.

No answer.

"He has left, he has left," I think. I try the door which is open, knock once again, and enter. The editor is sitting at his table, his face towards the window, pen in hand, about to write. When he hears my breathless greeting he turns half round, steals a quick look at me, shakes his head, and says:

"Oh, I haven't found time to read your sketch yet."

I am so delighted, because in that case he has not rejected it, that I answer:

"Oh, pray, sir, don't mention it. I quite understand—there is no hurry; in a few days, perhaps—"

"Yes, I shall see; besides, I have your address."

I forgot to inform him that I no longer had an address, and the interview is over. I bow myself out, and leave. Hope flames up again in me; as yet, nothing is lost—on the contrary, I might, for that matter, yet win all. And my brain began to spin a romance about a great council in Heaven, in which it had just been resolved that I should win—ay, triumphantly win ten shillings for a story.

If I only had some place in which to take refuge for the night! I consider where I can stow myself away, and am so absorbed in this query that I come to a standstill in the middle of the street. I forget where I am, and pose like a solitary beacon on a rock in mid-sea, whilst the tides rush and roar about it.

A newspaper boy offers me The Viking.

"It's real good value, sir!"

I look up and start; I am outside Semb's shop again. I quickly turn to the right-about, holding the parcel in front of me, and hurry down Kirkegaden, ashamed and afraid that any one might have seen me from the window. I pass by Ingebret's and the theatre, turn round by the box-office, and go towards the sea, near the fortress. I find a seat once more, and begin to consider afresh.

Where in the world shall I find a shelter for the night?

Was there a hole to be found where I could creep in and hide myself till morning? My pride forbade my returning to my lodging—besides, it could never really occur to me to go back on my word; I rejected this thought with great scorn, and I smiled superciliously as I thought of the little red rocking-chair. By some association of ideas, I find myself suddenly transported to a large, double room I once occupied in Haegdehaugen. I could see a tray on the table, filled with great slices of bread-and-butter. The vision changed; it was transformed into beef—a seductive piece of beef—a snow-white napkin, bread in plenty, a silver fork. The door opened; enter my landlady, offering me more tea....

Visions; senseless dreams! I tell myself that were I to get food now my head would become dizzy once more, fever would fill my brain, and I would have to fight again against many mad fancies. I could not stomach food, my inclination did not lie that way; that was peculiar to me—an idiosyncrasy of mine.

Maybe as night drew on a way could be found to procure shelter. There was no hurry; at the worst, I could seek a place out in the woods. I had the entire environs of the city at my disposal; as yet, there was no degree of cold worth speaking of in the weather.

And outside there the sea rocked in drowsy rest; ships and clumsy, broad-nosed prams ploughed graves in its bluish surface, and scattered rays to the right and left, and glided on, whilst the smoke rolled up in downy masses from the chimney-stacks, and the stroke of the engine pistons pierced the clammy air with a dull sound. There was no sun and no wind; the trees behind me were almost wet, and the seat upon which I sat was cold and damp.

Time went. I settled down to doze, waxed tired, and a little shiver ran down my back. A while after I felt that my eyelids began to droop, and I let them droop....

When I awoke it was dark all around me. I started up, bewildered and freezing. I seized my parcel and commenced to walk. I went faster and faster in order to get warm, slapped my arms, chafed my legs—which by now I could hardly feel under me—and thus reached the watch-house of the fire brigade. It was nine o'clock; I had been asleep for several hours.

Whatever shall I do with myself? I must go to some place. I stand there and stare up at the watch-house, and query if it would not be possible to succeed in getting into one of the passages if I were to watch for a moment when the watchman's back was turned. I ascend the steps, and prepare to open a conversation with the man. He lifts his ax in salute, and waits for what I may have to say. The uplifted ax, with its edge turned against me, darts like a cold slash through my nerves. I stand dumb with terror before this armed man, and draw involuntarily back. I say nothing, only glide farther and farther away from him. To save appearances I draw my hand over my forehead, as if I had forgotten something or other, and slink away. When I reached the pavement I felt as much saved as if I had just escaped a great peril, and I hurried away.

Cold and famished, more and more miserable in spirit, I flew up Carl Johann. I began to swear out aloud, troubling myself not a whit as to whether any one heard me or not. Arrived at Parliament House, just near the first trees, I suddenly, by some association of ideas, bethought myself of a young artist I knew, a stripling I had once saved from an assault in the Tivoli, and upon whom I had called later on. I snap my fingers gleefully, and wend my way to Tordenskjiolds Street, find the door, on which is fastened a card with C. Zacharias Bartel on it, and knock.

He came out himself, and smelt so fearfully of ale and tobacco that it was horrible.

"Good-evening!" I say.

"Good-evening! is that you? Now, why the deuce do you come so late? It doesn't look at all its best by lamplight. I have added a hayrick to it since, and have made a few other alterations. You must see it by daylight; there is no use our trying to see it now!"

"Let me have a look at it now, all the same," said I; though, for that matter, I did not in the least remember what picture he was talking about.

"Absolutely impossible," he replied; "the whole thing will look yellow; and, besides, there's another thing"—and he came towards me, whispering: "I have a little girl inside this evening, so it's clearly impracticable."

"Oh, in that case, of course there's no question about it."

I drew back, said good-night, and went away.

So there was no way out of it but to seek some place out in the woods. If only the fields were not so damp. I patted my blanket, and felt more and more at home at the thought of sleeping out. I had worried myself so long trying to find a shelter in town that I was wearied and bored with the whole affair. It would be a positive pleasure to get to rest, to resign myself; so I loaf down the street without thought in my head. At a place in Haegdehaugen I halted outside a provision shop where some food was displayed in the window. A cat lay there and slept beside a round French roll. There was a basin of lard and several basins of meal in the background. I stood a while and gazed at these eatables; but as I had no money wherewith to buy, I turned quickly away and continued my tramp. I went very slowly, passed by Majorstuen, went on, always on—it seemed to me for hours,—and came at length at Bogstad's wood.

I turned off the road here, and sat down to rest. Then I began to look about for a place to suit me, to gather together heather and juniper leaves, and make up a bed on a little declivity where it was a bit dry. I opened the parcel and took out the blanket; I was tired and exhausted with the long walk, and lay down at once. I turned and twisted many times before I could get settled. My ear pained me a little—it was slightly swollen from the whip-lash—and I could not lie on it. I pulled off my shoes and put them under my head, with the paper from Semb on top.

And the great spirit of darkness spread a shroud over me... everything was silent—everything. But up in the heights soughed the everlasting song, the voice of the air, the distant, toneless humming which is never silent. I listened so long to this ceaseless faint murmur that it began to bewilder me; it was surely a symphony from the rolling spheres above. Stars that intone a song....

"I am damned if it is, though," I exclaimed; and I laughed aloud to collect my wits. "They're night-owls hooting in Canaan!"

I rose again, pulled on my shoes, and wandered about in the gloom, only to lay down once more. I fought and wrestled with anger and fear until nearly dawn, then fell asleep at last.

It was broad daylight when I opened my eyes, and I had a feeling that it was going on towards noon.

I pulled on my shoes, packed up the blanket again, and set out for town. There was no sun to be seen today either; I shivered like a dog, my feet were benumbed, and water commenced to run from my eyes, as if they could not bear the daylight.

It was three o'clock. Hunger began to assail me downright in earnest. I was faint, and now and again I had to retch furtively. I swung round by the Dampkökken,[2] read the bill of fare, and shrugged my shoulders in a way to attract attention, as if corned beef or salt port was not meet food for me. After that I went towards the railway station.

A singular sense of confusion suddenly darted through my head. I stumbled on, determined not to heed it; but I grew worse and worse, and was forced at last to sit down on a step. My whole being underwent a change, as if something had slid aside in my inner self, or as if a curtain or tissue of my brain was rent in two.

I was not unconscious; I felt that my ear was gathering a little, and, as an acquaintance passed by, I recognized him at once and got up and bowed.

What sore of fresh, painful perception was this that was being added to the rest? Was it a consequence of sleeping in the sodden fields, or did it arise from my not having had any breakfast yet? Looking the whole thing squarely in the face, there was no meaning in

---

[2] Steam cooking-kitchen and famous cheap eating-house.

living on in this manner, by Christ's holy pains, there wasn't. I failed to see either how I had made myself deserving of this special persecution; and it suddenly entered my head that I might just as well turn rogue at once and go to my "Uncle's" with the blanket. I could pawn it for a shilling, and get three full meals, and so keep myself going until I thought of something else. 'Tis true I would have to swindle Hans Pauli. I was already on my way to the pawn-shop, but stopped outside the door, shook my head irresolutely, then turned back. The farther away I got the more gladsome, ay, delighted I became, that I had conquered this strong temptation. The consciousness that I was yet pure and honourable rose to my head, filled me with a splendid sense of having principle, character, of being a shining white beacon in a muddy, human sea amidst floating wreck.

Pawn another man's property for the sake of a meal, eat and drink one's self to perdition, brand one's soul with the first little scar, set the first black mark against one's honour, call one's self a blackguard to one's own face, and needs must cast one's eyes down before one's self? Never! never! It could never have been my serious intention—it had really never seriously taken hold of me; in fact, I could not be answerable for every loose, fleeting, desultory thought, particularly with such a headache as I had, and nearly killed carrying a blanket, too, that belonged to another fellow.

There would surely be some way or another of getting help when the right time came! Now, there was the grocer in Groenlandsleret. Had I importuned him every hour in the day since I sent in my application? Had I rung the bell early and late, and been turned away? Why, I had not even applied personally to him or sought an answer! It did not follow, surely, that it must needs be an absolutely vain attempt.

Maybe I had luck with me this time. Luck often took such a devious course, and I started for Groenlandsleret.

The last spasm that had darted through my head had exhausted me a little, and I walked very slowly and thought over what I would say to him.

Perhaps he was a good soul; if the whim seized him he might pay me for my work a shilling in advance, even without my asking for it. People of that sort had sometimes the most capital ideas.

I stole into a doorway and blackened the knees of my trousers with spittle to try and make them look a little respectable, left the parcel behind me in a dark corner at the back of a chest, and entered the little shop.

A man is standing pasting together bags made of old newspaper.

"I would like to see Mr. Christie," I said.

"That's me!" replied the man.

"Indeed!" Well, my name was so-and-so. I had taken the liberty of sending him an application, I did not know if it had been of any use.

He repeated my name a couple of times and commenced to laugh.

"Well now, you shall see," he said, taking my letter out of his breast-pocket, "if you will just be good enough to see how you deal with dates, sir. You dated your letter 1848," and the man roared with laughter.

"Yes, that was rather a mistake," I said, abashed—a distraction, a want of thought; I admitted it.

"You see I must have a man who, as a matter of fact, makes no mistakes in figures," said he. "I regret it, your handwriting is clear, and I like your letter, too, but—"

I waited a while; this could not possibly be the man's final say. He busied himself again with the bags.

"Yes, it was a pity," I said; "really an awful pity, but of course it would not occur again; and, after all, surely this little error could not have rendered me quite unfit to keep books?"

"No, I didn't say that," he answered, "but in the meantime it had so much weight with me that I decided at once upon another man."

"So the place is filled?"

"Yes."

"A—h, well, then there's nothing more to be said about it!"

"No! I'm sorry, but—"

"Good-evening!" said I.

Fury welled up in me, blazing with brutal strength. I fetched my parcel from the entry, set my teeth together, jostled against the peaceful folk on the footpath, and never once asked their pardon.

As one man stopped and set me to rights rather sharply for my behaviour, I turned round and screamed a single meaningless word in his ear, clenched my fist right under his nose, and stumbled on, hardened by a blind rage that I could not control.

He called a policeman, and I desired nothing better than to have one between my hands just for one moment. I slackened my pace intentionally in order to give him an opportunity of overtaking me; but he did not come. Was there now any reason whatever that absolutely every one of one's most earnest and most persevering efforts should fail? Why, too, had I written 1828? In what way did that infernal date concern me? Here I was going about starving, so that my entrails wriggle together in me like worms, and it was, as far as I knew, not decreed in the book of fate that anything in the shape of food would turn up later on in the day.

I was becoming mentally and physically more and more prostrate; I was letting myself down each day to less and less honest actions, so that I lied on each day without blushing, cheated poor people out of their rent, struggled with the meanest thoughts of making away with other men's blankets—all without remorse or prick of conscience.

Foul places began to gather in my inner being, black spores which spread more and more. And up in Heaven God Almighty sat and kept a watchful eye on me, and took heed that my destruction proceeded in accordance with all the rules of art, uniformly and gradually, without a break in the measure.

But in the abysses of hell the angriest devils bristled with range because it lasted such a long time until I committed a mortal sin, an unpardonable offence for which God in His justice must cast me—down....

I quickened my pace, hurried faster and faster, turned suddenly to the left and found myself, excited and angry, in a light ornate doorway. I did not pause, not for one second, but the whole peculiar ornamentation of the entrance struck on my perception in a flash; every detail of the decoration and the tiling of the floor stood clear on my mental vision as I sprang up the stairs. I rang violently on the second floor. Why should I stop exactly on the second floor? And why just seize hold of this bell which was some little way from the stairs?

A young lady in a grey gown with black trimming came out and opened the door. She looked for a moment in astonishment at me, then shook her head and said:

"No, we have not got anything today," and she made a feint to close the door.

What induced me to thrust myself in this creature's way? She took me without further ado for a beggar.

I got cool and collected at once. I raised my hat, made a respectful bow, and, as if I had not caught her words, said, with the utmost politeness:

"I hope you will excuse me, madam, for ringing so hard, the bell was new to me. Is it not here that an invalid gentleman lives who has advertised for a man to wheel him about in a chair?"

She stood awhile and digested this mendacious invention and seemed to be irresolute in her summing up of my person.

"No!" she said at length; "no, there is no invalid gentleman living here."

"Not really? An elderly gentleman—two hours a day—sixpence an hour?"

"No!"

"Ah! in that case, I again ask pardon," said I. "It is perhaps on the first floor. I only wanted, in any case, to recommend a man I know, in whom I am interested; my name is Wedel-Jarlsberg,"[3] and I bowed again and drew back. The young lady blushed crimson, and in her embarrassment could not stir from the spot, but stood and stared after me as I descended the stairs.

My calm had returned to me, and my head was clear. The lady's

---

[3] The last family bearing title of nobility in Norway.

saying that she had nothing for me today had acted upon me like an icy shower. So it had gone so far with me that any one might point at me, and say to himself, "There goes a beggar—one of those people who get their food handed out to them at folk's back-doors!"

I halted outside an eating-house in Möller Street, and sniffed the fresh smell of meat roasting inside; my hand was already upon the door-handle, and I was on the point of entering without any fixed purpose, when I bethought myself in time, and left the spot. On reaching the market, and seeking for a place to rest for a little, I found all the benches occupied, and I sought in vain all round outside the church for a quiet seat, where I could sit down.

Naturally, I told myself, gloomily—naturally, naturally; and I commenced to walk again. I took a turn round the fountain at the corner of the bazaar, and swallowed a mouthful of water. On again, dragging one foot after the other; stopped for a long time before each shop window; halted, and watched every vehicle that drove by. I felt a scorching heat in my head, and something pulsated strangely in my temples. The water I had drunk disagreed with me fearfully, and I retched, stopping here and there to escape being noticed in the open street. In this manner I came up to Our Saviour's Cemetery.

I sat down here, with my elbows on my knees and my head in my hands. In this cramped position I was more at ease, and I no longer felt the little gnawing in my chest.

A stone-cutter lay on his stomach on a large slab of granite, at the side of me, and cut inscriptions. He had blue spectacles on, and reminded me of an acquaintance of mine, whom I had almost forgotten.

If I could only knock all shame on the head and apply to him. Tell him the truth right out, that things were getting awfully tight with me now; ay, that I found it hard enough to keep alive. I could give him my shaving-tickets.

Zounds! my shaving-tickets; tickets for nearly a shilling. I search nervously for this precious treasure. As I do not find them quickly enough, I spring to my feet and search, in a sweat of fear. I discover them at last in the bottom of my breast-pocket, together with other papers—some clean, some written on—of no value.

I count these six tickets over many times, backwards and forwards; I had not much use for them; it might pass for a whim—a notion of mine—that I no longer cared to get shaved.

I was saved to the extent of sixpence—a white sixpence of Kongsberg silver. The bank closed at six; I could watch for my man outside the Opland Café between seven and eight.

I sat, and was for a long time pleased with this thought. Time went. The wind blew lustily through the chestnut trees around me, and the day declined.

After all, was it not rather petty to come slinking up with six shaving-tickets to a young gentleman holding a good position in a bank? Perhaps, he had already a book, maybe two, quite full of spick and span tickets, a contrast to the crumpled ones I held.

Who could tell? I felt in all my pockets for anything else I could let go with them, but found nothing. If I could only offer him my tie? I could well do without it if I buttoned my coat tightly up, which, by the way, I was already obliged to do, as I had no waistcoat. I untied it—it was a large overlapping bow which hid half my chest,—brushed it carefully, and folded it up in a piece of clean white writing-paper, together with the tickets. Then I left the churchyard and took the road leading to the Opland.

It was seven by the Town Hall clock. I walked up and down hard by the café, kept close to the iron railings, and kept a sharp watch on all who went in and came out of the door. At last, about eight o'clock, I saw the young fellow, fresh, elegantly dressed, coming up the hill and across to the cafe door. My heart fluttered like a little bird in my breast as I caught sight of him, and I blurted out, without even a greeting:

"Sixpence, old friend!" I said, putting on cheek; "here is the worth of it," and I thrust the little packet into his hand.

"Haven't got it," he exclaimed. "God knows if I have!" and he turned his purse inside out right before my eyes. "I was out last night and got totally cleared out! You must believe me, I literally haven't got it."

"No, no, my dear fellow; I suppose it is so," I answered, and I took his word for it. There was, indeed, no reason why he should lie about such a trifling matter. It struck me, too, that his blue eyes were moist whilst he ransacked his pockets and found nothing. I drew back. "Excuse me," I said; "it was only just that I was a bit hard up." I was already a piece down the street, when he called after me about the little packet. "Keep it! keep it," I answered; "you are welcome to it. There are only a few trifles in it—a bagatelle; about all I own in the world," and I became so touched at my own words, they sounded so pathetic in the twilight, that I fell a-weeping....

The wind freshened, the clouds chased madly across the heavens, and it grew cooler and cooler as it got darker. I walked, and cried as I walked, down the whole street; felt more and more commiseration with myself, and repeated, time after time, a few words, an ejaculation, which called forth fresh tears whenever they were on the point of ceasing: "Lord God, I feel so wretched! Lord God, I feel so wretched!"

An hour passed; passed with such strange slowness, such weariness. I spent a long time in Market Street; sat on steps, stole into doorways, and when any one approached, stood and stared absently into the shops where people bustled about with wares or money. At last I found myself a sheltered place, behind a deal hoarding, between the church and the bazaar.

No; I couldn't go out into the woods again this evening. Things must take their course. I had not strength enough to go, and it was such an endless way there. I would kill the night as best I could, and remain where I was; if it got all too cold, well, I could walk round the church. I would not in any case worry myself any more about that, and I leant back and dozed.

The noise around me diminished; the shops closed. The steps of the pedestrians sounded more and more rarely, and in all the windows about the lights went out. I opened my eyes, and became aware of a figure standing in front of me. The flash of shining buttons told me it was a policeman, though I could not see the man's face.

"Good-night," he said.

"Good-night," I answered and got afraid.

"Where do you live?" he queried.

I name, from habit, and without thought, my old address, the little attic.

He stood for a while.

"Have I done anything wrong?" I asked anxiously.

"No, not at all!" he replied; "but you had perhaps better be getting home now; it's cold lying here."

"Ay, that's true; I feel it is a little chilly." I said good-night, and instinctively took the road to my old abode. If I only set about it carefully, I might be able to get upstairs without being heard; there were eight steps in all, and only the two top ones creaked under my tread. Down at the door I took off my shoes, and ascended. It was quiet everywhere. I could hear the slow tick-tack of a clock, and a child crying a little. After that I heard nothing. I found my door, lifted the latch as I was accustomed to do, entered the room, and shut the door noiselessly after me.

Everything was as I had left it. The curtains were pulled aside from the windows, and the bed stood empty. I caught a glimpse of a note lying on the table; perhaps it was my note to the landlady—she might never have been up here since I went away.

I fumbled with my hands over the white spot, and felt, to my astonishment, that it was a letter. I take it over to the window, examine as well as it is possible in the dark the badly-written letters of the address, and make out at least my own name. Ah, I thought, an answer from my landlady, forbidding me to enter the room again if I were for sneaking back.

Slowly, quite slowly I left the room, carrying my shoes in one hand, the letter in the other, and the blanket under my arm. I draw myself up, set my teeth as I tread on the creaking steps, get happily down the stairs, and stand once more at the door. I put on my shoes, take my time with the laces, sit a while quietly after I'm ready, and stare vacantly before me, holding the letter in my hand. Then I get up and go.

The flickering ray of a gas lamp gleams up the street. I make straight for the light, lean my parcel against the lamp-post and open the letter. All this with the utmost deliberation. A stream of light, as it were, darts through my breast, and I hear that I give a little cry—a meaningless sound of joy. The letter was from the editor. My story was accepted—had been set in type immediately, straight off! A few slight alterations.... A couple of errors in writing amended.... Worked out with talent ... be printed tomorrow ... half-a-sovereign.

I laughed and cried, took to jumping and running down the street, stopped, slapped my thighs, swore loudly and solemnly into space at nothing in particular. And time went.

All through the night until the bright dawn I "jodled" about the streets and repeated—"Worked out with talent—therefore a little masterpiece—a stroke of genius—and half-a-sovereign."

Part II

A few weeks later I was out one evening. Once more I had sat out in a churchyard and worked at an article for one of the newspapers. But whilst I was struggling with it eight o'clock struck, and darkness closed in, and time for shutting the gates.

I was hungry—very hungry. The ten shillings had, worse luck, lasted all too short. It was now two, ay, nearly three days since I had eaten anything, and I felt somewhat faint; holding the pencil even had taxed me a little. I had half a penknife and a bunch of keys in my pocket, but not a farthing.

When the churchyard gate shut I meant to have gone straight home, but, from an instinctive dread of my room—a vacant tinker's workshop, where all was dark and barren, and which, in fact, I had got permission to occupy for the present—I stumbled on, passed, not caring where I went, the Town Hall, right to the sea, and over to a scat near the railway bridge.

At this moment not a sad thought troubled me. I forgot my distress, and felt calmed by the view of the sea, which lay peaceful and lovely in the murkiness. For old habit's sake I would please myself by reading through the bit I had just written, and which seemed to my suffering head the best thing I had ever done.

I took my manuscript out of my pocket to try and decipher it, held it close up to my eyes, and ran through it, one line after the other. At last I got tired, and put the papers back in my pocket. Everything was still. The sea stretched away in pearly blueness, and little birds flitted noiselessly by me from place to place.

A policeman patrols in the distance; otherwise there is not a soul visible, and the whole harbour is hushed in quiet.

I count my belongings once more—half a penknife, a bunch of keys, but not a farthing. Suddenly I dive into my pocket and take the papers out again. It was a mechanical movement, an unconscious nervous twitch. I selected a white unwritten page, and—God knows where I got the notion from—but I made a cornet, closed it carefully, so that it looked as if it were filled with something, and threw it far out on to the pavement. The breeze blew it onward a little, and then it lay still.

By this time hunger had begun to assail me in earnest. I sat and looked at the white paper cornet, which seemed as if it might be bursting with shining silver pieces, and incited myself to believe that it really did contain something. I sat and coaxed myself quite audibly to guess the sum; if I guessed aright, it was to be mine.

I imagined the tiny, pretty penny bits at the bottom and the thick fluted shillings on top—a whole paper cornet full of money! I sat and gazed at it with wide opened eyes, and urged myself to go and steal it.

Then I hear the constable cough. What puts it into my head to do the same? I rise up from the seat and repeat the cough three times so that he may hear it. Won't he jump at the corner when he comes. I sat and laughed at this trick, rubbed my hands with glee, and swore with rollicking recklessness. What a disappointment he will get, the dog! Wouldn't this piece of villainy make him inclined to sink into hell's hottest pool of torment! I was drunk with starvation; my hunger had made me tipsy.

A few minutes later the policeman comes by, clinking his iron heels on the pavement, peering on all sides. He takes his time; he has the whole night before him; he does not notice the paper bag—not till he comes quite close to it. Then he stops and stares at it. It looks so white and so full as it lies there; perhaps a little sum—what? A little sum of silver money?... and he picks it up. Hum ... it is light—very light; maybe an expensive feather; some hat trimming.... He opened it carefully with his big hands, and looked in. I laughed, laughed, slapped my thighs, and laughed, like a maniac. And not a sound issued from my throat; my laughter was hushed and feverish to the intensity of tears.

Clink, clink again over the paving-stones, and the policeman took a turn towards the landing-stage. I sat there, with tears in my eyes, and hiccoughed for breath, quite beside myself with feverish merriment. I commenced to talk aloud to myself all about the cornet, imitated the poor policeman's movements, peeped into my hollow hand, and repeated over and over again to myself, "He coughed as he threw it away—he coughed as he threw it away." I added new words to these, gave them additional point, changed the whole sentence, and made it catching and piquant. He coughed once—Kheu heu!

I exhausted myself in weaving variations on these words, and the evening was far advanced before my mirth ceased. Then a drowsy quiet overcame me; a pleasant languor which I did not attempt to resist. The darkness had intensified, and a slight breeze furrowed the pearl-blue sea. The ships, the masts of which I could see outlined against the sky, looked with their black hulls like voiceless monsters that bristled and lay in wait for me. I had no pain—my hunger had taken the edge off it. In its stead I felt pleasantly empty, untouched by everything around me, and glad not to be noticed by any one. I put my feet up on the seat and leant back. Thus I could best appreciate the well-being of perfect isolation. There was not a cloud on my mind, not a feeling of discomfort, and so far as my thought reached, I had not a whim, not a desire unsatisfied. I lay with open eyes, in a state of utter absence of mind. I felt myself charmed away. Moreover, not a sound disturbed me. Soft darkness had hidden the whole world from my sight, and buried me in ideal rest. Only the lonely, crooning voice of silence strikes in monotones on my ear, and the dark monsters out there will draw me to them when night comes, and they will bear me far across the sea, through strange lands where no man dwells, and they will bear me to Princess Ylajali's palace, where an undreamt-of grandeur awaits me, greater than that of any other man. And she herself will be sitting in a dazzling hall where all is amethyst, on a throne of yellow roses, and will stretch out her hands to me when I alight; will smile and call as I approach and kneel: "Welcome, welcome, knight, to me and my land! I have waited twenty summers for you, and called for you on all bright nights. And when you sorrowed I have wept here, and when you slept I have breathed sweet dreams in you!"... And the fair one clasps my hand and, holding it, leads me through long corridors where great crowds of people cry, "Hurrah!" through bright gardens where three hundred tender maidens laugh and play; and through another hall where all is of emerald; and here the sun shines.

In the corridors and galleries choirs of musicians march by, and rills of perfume are wafted towards me.

I clasp her hand in mine; I feel the wild witchery of enchantment shiver through my blood, and I fold my arms around her, and she whispers, "Not here; come yet farther!" and we enter a crimson room, where all is of ruby, a foaming glory, in which I faint.

Then I feel her arms encircle me; her breath fans my face with a whispered "Welcome, loved one! Kiss me ... more ... more...."

I see from my seat stars shooting before my eyes, and my thoughts are swept away in a hurricane of light....

I had fallen asleep where I lay, and was awakened by the policeman. There I sat, recalled mercilessly to life and misery. My first feeling was of stupid amazement at finding myself in the open air; but this was quickly replaced by a bitter despondency, I was near crying with sorrow at being still alive. It had rained whilst I slept, and my clothes were soaked through and through, and I felt a damp cold in my limbs.

The darkness was denser; it was with difficulty that I could distinguish the policeman's face in front of me.

"So, that's right," he said; "get up now."

I got up at once; if he had commanded me to lie down again I would have obeyed too. I was fearfully dejected, and utterly without strength; added to that, I was almost instantly aware of the pangs of hunger again.

"Hold on there!" the policeman shouted after me; "why, you're walking off without your hat, you Juggins! So—h there; now, go on."

"I indeed thought there was something—something I had forgotten," I stammered, absently. "Thanks, good-night!" and I stumbled away.

If one only had a little bread to eat; one of those delicious little brown loaves that one could bite into as one walked along the street; and as I went on I thought over the particular sort of brown bread that would be so unspeakably good to munch. I was bitterly hungry; wished myself dead and buried; I got maudlin, and wept.

There never was any end to my misery. Suddenly I stopped in the street, stamped on the pavement, and cursed loudly. What was it he called me? A "Juggins"? I would just show him what calling me a "Juggins" means. I turned round and ran back. I felt red-hot with anger. Down the street I stumbled, and fell, but I paid no heed to it, jumped up again, and ran on. But by the time I reached the railway station I had become so tired that I did not feel able to proceed all the way to the landing-stage; besides, my anger had cooled down with the run. At length I pulled up and drew breath. Was it not, after all, a matter of perfect indifference to me what such a policeman said? Yes; but one couldn't stand everything. Right enough, I interrupted myself; but he knew no better. And I found this argument satisfactory. I repeated twice to myself, "He knew no better"; and with that I returned again.

"Good Lord!" thought I, wrathfully, "what things you do take into your head: running about like a madman through the soaking wet streets on dark nights." My hunger was now tormenting me excruciatingly, and gave me no rest. Again and again I swallowed saliva to try and satisfy myself a little; I fancied it helped.

I had been pinched, too, for food for ever so many weeks before this last period set in, and my strength had diminished considerably of late. When I had been lucky enough to raise five shillings by some manoeuvre or another they only lasted any time with difficulty; not long enough for me to be restored to health before a new hunger period set in and reduced me again. My back and shoulders caused me the worst trouble. I could stop the little gnawing I had in my chest by coughing hard, or bending well forward as I walked, but I had no remedy for back and shoulders. Whatever was the reason that things would not brighten up for me? Was I not just as much entitled to live as any one else? for example, as Bookseller Pascha or Steam Agent Hennechen? Had I not two shoulders like a giant, and two strong hands to work with? and had I not, in sooth, even applied for a place as wood-chopper in Möllergaden in order to earn my daily bread? Was I lazy? Had I not applied for situations, attended lectures, written articles, and worked day and night like a man possessed? Had I not lived like a miser, eaten bread and milk when I had plenty, bread alone when I had little, and starved when I had nothing? Did I live in an hotel? Had I a suite of rooms on the first floor? Why, I am living in a loft over a tinker's workshop, a loft already forsaken by God and man last winter, because the snow blew in. So I could not understand the whole thing; not a bit of it.

I slouched on, and dwelt upon all this, and there was not as much as a spark of bitterness or malice or envy in my mind.

I halted at a paint-shop and gazed into the window. I tried to read the labels on a couple of the tins, but it was too dark. Vexed with myself over this new whim, and excited—almost angry at not being able to make out what these tins held,—I rapped twice sharply on the window and went on.

Up the street I saw a policeman. I quickened my pace, went close up to him, and said, without the slightest provocation, "It is ten o'clock."

"No, it's two," he answered, amazed.

"No, it's ten," I persisted; "it is ten o'clock!" and, groaning with anger, I stepped yet a pace or two nearer, clenched my fist, and said, "Listen, do you know what, it's ten o'clock!"

He stood and considered a while, summed up my appearance, stared aghast at me, and at last said, quite gently, "In any case, it's about time ye were getting home. Would ye like me to go with ye a bit?"

I was completely disarmed by this man's unexpected friendliness. I felt that tears sprang to my eyes, and I hastened to reply:

"No, thank you! I have only been out a little too late in a café. Thank you very much all the same!"

He saluted with his hand to his helmet as I turned away. His friendliness had overwhelmed me, and I cried weakly, because I had not even a little coin to give him.

I halted, and looked after him as he went slowly on his way. I struck my forehead, and, in measure, as he disappeared from my sight, I cried more violently.

I railed at myself for my poverty, called myself abusive names, invented furious designations—rich, rough nuggets—in a vein of abuse with which I overwhelmed myself. I kept on at this until I was nearly home. On coming to the door I discovered I had dropped my keys.

"Oh, of course," I muttered to myself, "why shouldn't I lose my keys? Here I am, living in a yard where there is a stable underneath and a tinker's workshop up above. The door is locked at night, and no one, no one can open it; therefore, why should I not lose my keys?

"I am as wet as a dog—a little hungry—ah, just ever such a little hungry, and slightly, ay, absurdly tired about my knees; therefore, why should I not lose them?

"Why, for that matter, had not the whole house flitted out to Aker by the time I came home and wished to enter it?" ... and I laughed to myself, hardened by hunger and exhaustion.

I could hear the horses stamp in the stables, and I could see my window above, but I could not open the door, and I could not get in.

It had begun to rain again, and I felt the water soak through to my shoulders. At the Town Hall I was seized by a bright idea. I would ask the policeman to open the door. I applied at once to a constable, and earnestly begged him to accompany me and let me in, if he could.

Yes, if he could, yes! But he couldn't; he had no key. The police keys were not there; they were kept in the Detective Department.

What was I to do then?

Well, I could go to an hotel and get a bed!

But I really couldn't go to an hotel and get a bed; I had not money, I had been out—in a café ... he knew....

We stood a while on the Town Hall steps. He considered and examined my personal appearance. The rain fell in torrents outside.

"Well then, you must go to the guard-house and report yourself as homeless!" said he.

Homeless? I hadn't thought of that. Yes, by Jove, that was a capital idea; and I thanked the constable on the spot for the suggestion. Could I simply go in and say I was homeless?

"Just that."...

"Your name?" inquired the guard.

"Tangen—Andreas Tangen!"

I don't know why I lied; my thoughts fluttered about disconnectedly and inspired me with many singular whims, more than I knew what to do with. I hit upon this out-of-the-way name on the spur of the moment, and blurted it out without any calculation. I lied without any occasion for doing so.

"Occupation?"

This was driving me into a corner with a vengeance. Occupation! what was my occupation? I thought first of turning myself into a tinker—but I dared not; firstly, I had given myself a name that was not common to every and any tinker—besides, I wore pince-nez. It suddenly entered my head to be foolhardy. I took a step forward and said firmly, almost solemnly:

"A journalist."

The guard gave a start before he wrote it down, whilst I stood as important as a homeless Cabinet Minister before the barrier. It roused no suspicions. The guard understood quite well why I hesitated a little before answering. What did it look like to see a journalist in the night guard-house without a roof over his head?

"On what paper, Herr Tangen?"

"Morgenbladet!" said I. "I have been out a little too late this evening, more's the shame!"

"Oh, we won't mention that," he interrupted, with a smile; "when young people are out ... we understand!"

Turning to a policeman, he said, as he rose and bowed politely to me, "Show this gentleman up to the reserved section. Good-night!"

I felt ice run down my back at my own boldness, and I clenched my hands to steady myself a bit. If I only hadn't dragged in the Morgenbladet. I knew Friele could show his teeth when he liked, and I was reminded of that by the grinding of the key turning in the lock.

"The gas will burn for ten minutes," remarked the policeman at the door.

"And then does it go out?"

"Then it goes out!"

I sat on the bed and listened to the turning of the key. The bright cell had a friendly air; I felt comfortably and well sheltered; and listened with pleasure to the rain outside—I couldn't wish myself anything better than such a cosy cell. My contentment increased. Sitting on the bed, hat in hand, and with eyes fastened on the gas jet over in the wall, I gave myself up to thinking over the minutes of my first interview with the police. This was the first time, and how hadn't I fooled them? "Journalist!—Tangen! if you please! and then Morgenbladet!" Didn't I appeal straight to his heart with Morgenbladet? "We won't mention that! Eh? Sat in state in the Stiftsgaarden till two o'clock; forgot door-key and a pocket-book with a thousand kroner at home. Show this gentleman up to the reserved section!"...

All at once out goes the gas with a strange suddenness, without diminishing or flickering.

I sit in the deepest darkness; I cannot see my hand, nor the white walls— nothing. There was nothing for it but to go to bed, and I undressed.

But I was not tired from want of sleep, and it would not come to me. I lay a while gazing into the darkness, this dense mass of gloom that had no bottom—my thoughts could not fathom it.

It seemed beyond all measure dense to me, and I felt its presence oppress me. I closed my eyes, commenced to sing under my breath, and tossed to and fro, in order to distract myself, but to no purpose. The darkness had taken possession of my thoughts and left me not a moment in peace. Supposing I were myself to be absorbed in darkness; made one with it?

I raise myself up in bed and fling out my arms. My nervous condition has got the upper hand of me, and nothing availed, no matter how much I tried to work against it. There I sat, a prey to the most singular fantasies, listening to myself crooning lullabies, sweating with the exertion of striving to hush myself to rest. I peered into the gloom, and I never in all the days of my life felt such darkness. There was no doubt that I found myself here, in face of a peculiar kind of darkness; a desperate element to which no one had hitherto paid attention. The most ludicrous thoughts busied me, and everything made me afraid.

A little hole in the wall at the head of my bed occupies me greatly—a nail hole. I find the marks in the wall—I feel it, blow into it, and try to guess its depth. That was no innocent hole—not at all. It was a downright intricate and mysterious hole, which I must guard against! Possessed by the thought of this hole, entirely beside myself with curiosity and fear, I get out of bed and seize hold of my penknife in order to gauge its depth, and convince myself that it does not reach right into the next wall.

I lay down once more to try and fall asleep, but in reality to wrestle again with the darkness. The rain had ceased outside, and I could not hear a sound. I continued for a long time to listen for footsteps in the street, and got no peace until I heard a pedestrian go by—to judge from the sound, a constable. Suddenly I snap my fingers many times and laugh: "That was the very deuce! Ha—ha!" I imagined I had discovered a new word. I rise up in bed and say, "It is not in the language; I have discovered it. 'Kuboa.' It has letters as a word has. By the benign God, man, you have discovered a word!... 'Kuboa' ... a word of profound import."

I sit with open eyes, amazed at my own find, and laugh for joy. Then I begin to whisper; some one might spy on me, and I intended to keep my discovery a secret. I entered into the joyous frenzy of hunger. I was empty and free from pain, and I gave free rein to my thoughts.

In all calmness I revolve things in my mind. With the most singular jerks in my chain of ideas I seek to explain the meaning of my new word. There was no occasion for it to mean either God or the Tivoli;[4] and who said that it was to signify cattle show? I clench my hands fiercely, and repeat once again, "Who said that it was to signify cattle show?" No; on second thoughts, it was not absolutely necessary that it should mean padlock, or sunrise. It was not difficult to find a meaning for such a word as this. I would wait and see. In the meantime I could sleep on it.

I lie there on the stretcher-bed and laugh slyly, but say nothing;

---

[4] Theatre of Varieties, etc., and Garden in Christiania.

give vent to no opinion one way or the other. Some minutes pass over, and I wax nervous; this new word torments me unceasingly, returns again and again, takes up my thoughts, and makes me serious. I had fully formed an opinion as to what it should not signify, but had come to no conclusion as to what it should signify. "That is quite a matter of detail," I said aloud to myself, and I clutched my arm and reiterated: "That is quite a matter of detail." The word was found, God be praised! and that was the principal thing. But ideas worry me without end and hinder me from falling asleep. Nothing seemed good enough to me for this unusually rare word. At length I sit up in bed again, grasp my head in both hands, and say, "No! it is just this, it is impossible to let it signify emigration or tobacco factory. If it could have meant anything like that I would have decided upon it long since and taken the consequences." No; in reality the word is fitted to signify something psychical, a feeling, a state. Could I not apprehend it? and I reflect profoundly in order to find something psychical. Then it seems to me that some one is interposing, interrupting my confab. I answer angrily, "Beg pardon! Your match in idiocy is not to be found; no, sir! Knitting cotton? Ah! go to hell!" Well, really I had to laugh. Might I ask why should I be forced to let it signify knitting cotton, when I had a special dislike to its signifying knitting cotton? I had discovered the word myself, so, for that matter, I was perfectly within my right in letting it signify whatsoever I pleased. As far as I was aware, I had not yet expressed an opinion as to....

But my brain got more and more confused. At last I sprang out of bed to look for the water-tap. I was not thirsty, but my head was in a fever, and I felt an instinctive longing for water. When I had drunk some I got into bed again, and determined with all my might to settle to sleep. I closed my eyes and forced myself to keep quiet. I lay thus for some minutes without making a movement, sweated and felt my blood jerk violently through my veins. No, it was really too delicious the way he thought to find money in the paper cornet! He only coughed once, too! I wonder if he is pacing up and down there yet! Sitting on my bench? the pearly blue sea ... the ships....

I opened my eyes; how could I keep them shut when I could not sleep? The same darkness brooded over me; the same unfathomable black eternity which my thoughts strove against and could not understand. I made the most despairing efforts to find a word black enough to characterize this darkness; a word so horribly black that it would darken my lips if I named it. Lord! how dark it was! and I am carried back in thought to the sea and the dark monsters that lay in wait for me. They would draw me to them, and clutch me tightly and bear me away by land and sea, through dark realms that no soul has seen. I feel myself on board, drawn through waters, hovering in clouds, sinking—sinking.

I give a hoarse cry of terror, clutch the bed tightly—I had made such a perilous journey, whizzing down through space like a bolt. Oh, did I not feel that I was saved as I struck my hands against the wooden frame! “This is the way one dies!” said I to myself. “Now you will die!” and I lay for a while and thought over that I was to die.

Then I start up in bed and ask severely, “If I found the word, am I not absolutely within my right to decide myself what it is to signify?”... I could hear myself that I was raving. I could hear it now whilst I was talking. My madness was a delirium of weakness and prostration, but I was not out of my senses. All at once the thought darted through my brain that I was insane. Seized with terror, I spring out of bed again, I stagger to the door, which I try to open, fling myself against it a couple of times to burst it, strike my head against the wall, bewail loudly, bite my fingers, cry and curse....

All was quiet; only my own voice echoed from the walls. I had fallen to the floor, incapable of stumbling about the cell any longer.

Lying there I catch a glimpse, high up, straight before my eyes, of a greyish square in the wall, a suggestion of white, a presage—it must be of daylight. I felt it must be daylight, felt it through every pore in my body. Oh, did I not draw a breath of delighted relief! I flung myself flat on the floor and cried for very joy over this blessed glimpse of light, sobbed for very gratitude, blew a kiss to the window, and conducted myself like a maniac. And at this moment I was perfectly conscious of what I was doing. All my dejection had vanished; all despair and pain had ceased, and I had at this moment, at least as far as my thought reached, not a wish unfilled. I sat up on the floor, folded my hands, and waited patiently for the dawn.

What a night this had been!

That they had not heard any noise! I thought with astonishment. But then I was in the reserved section, high above all the prisoners. A homeless Cabinet Minister, if I might say so.

Still in the best of humours, with eyes turned towards the lighter, ever lighter square in the wall, I amused myself acting Cabinet Minister; called myself Von Tangen, and clothed my speech in a dress of red-tape. My fancies had not ceased, but I was far less nervous. If I only had not been thoughtless enough to leave my pocket-book at home! Might I not have the honour of assisting his Right Honourable the Prime Minister to bed? And in all seriousness, and with much ceremony I went over to the stretcher and lay down.

By this it was so light that I could distinguish in some degree the outlines of the cell and, little by little, the heavy handle of the door. This diverted me; the monotonous darkness so irritating in its impenetrability that it prevented me from seeing myself was broken; my blood flowed more quietly; I soon felt my eyes close.

I was aroused by a couple of knocks on my door. I jumped up in all haste, and clad myself hurriedly; my clothes were still wet through from last night.

"You'll report yourself downstairs to the officer on duty," said the constable.

Were there more formalities to be gone through, then? I thought with fear.

Below I entered a large room, where thirty or forty people sat, all homeless. They were called up one by one by the registering clerk, and one by one they received a ticket for breakfast. The officer on duty repeated constantly to the policeman at his side, "Did he get a ticket? Don't forget to give them tickets; they look as if they wanted a meal!"

And I stood and looked at these tickets, and wished I had one.

"Andreas Tangen—journalist."

I advanced and bowed.

"But, my dear fellow, how did you come here?"

I explained the whole state of the case, repeated the same story as last night, lied without winking, lied with frankness—had been out rather late, worse luck ... café ... lost door-key....

"Yes," he said, and he smiled; "that's the way! Did you sleep well then?"

I answered, "Like a Cabinet Minister—like a Cabinet Minister!"

"I am glad to hear it," he said, and he stood up. "Good-morning."

And I went!

A ticket! a ticket for me too! I have not eaten for more than three long days and nights. A loaf! But no one offered me a ticket, and I dared not demand one. It would have roused suspicion at once. They would begin to poke their noses into my private affairs, and discover who I really was; they might arrest me for false pretences; and so, with elevated head, the carriage of a millionaire, and hands thrust under my coat-tails, I stride out of the guard-house.

The sun shone warmly, early as it was. It was ten o'clock, and the traffic in Young's Market was in full swing. Which way should I take? I slapped my pockets and felt for my manuscript. At eleven I would try and see the editor. I stand a while on the balustrade, and watch the bustle under me. Meanwhile, my clothes commenced to steam. Hunger put in its appearance afresh, gnawed at my breast, clutched me, and gave small, sharp stabs that caused me pain.

Had I not a friend—an acquaintance whom I could apply to? I ransack my memory to find a man good for a penny piece, and fail to find him.

Well, it was a lovely day, anyway! Sunlight bright and warm surrounded me. The sky stretched away like a beautiful sea over the Lier mountains.

Without knowing it, I was on my way home. I hungered sorely. I found a chip of wood in the street to chew—that helped a bit. To think that I hadn't thought of that sooner! The door was open; the stable-boy bade me good-morning as usual.

"Fine weather," said he.

"Yes," I replied. That was all I found to say. Could I ask for the loan of a shilling? He would be sure to lend it willingly if he could; besides that, I had written a letter for him once.

He stood and turned something over in his mind before he ventured on saying it.

"Fine weather! Ahem! I ought to pay my landlady today; you wouldn't be so kind as to lend me five shillings, would you? Only for a few days, sir. You did me a service once before, so you did."

"No; I really can't do it, Jens Olaj," I answered. "Not now—perhaps later on, maybe in the afternoon," and I staggered up the stairs to my room.

I flung myself on my bed, and laughed. How confoundedly lucky it was that he had forestalled me; my self-respect was saved. Five shillings! God bless you, man, you might just as well have asked me for five shares in the Dampkökken, or an estate out in Aker.

And the thought of these five shillings made me laugh louder and louder. Wasn't I a devil of a fellow, eh? Five shillings! My mirth increased, and I gave way to it. Ugh! what a shocking smell of cooking there was here—a downright disgustingly strong smell of chops for dinner, phew! and I flung open the window to let out this beastly smell. "Waiter, a plate of beef!" Turning to the table —this miserable table that I was forced to support with my knees when I wrote—I bowed profoundly, and said:

"May I ask will you take a glass of wine? No? I am Tangen—Tangen, the Cabinet Minister. I—more's the pity—I was out a little late ... the door-key." Once more my thoughts ran without rein in intricate paths. I was continually conscious that I talked at random, and yet I gave utterance to no word without hearing and understanding it. I said to myself, "Now you are talking at random again," and yet I could not help myself. It was as if one were lying awake, and yet talking in one's sleep.

My head was light, without pain and without pressure, and my mood was unshadowed. It sailed away with me, and I made no effort.

"Come in! Yes, only come right in! As you see everything is of ruby—Ylajali, Ylajali! that swelling crimson silken divan! Ah, how passionately she breathes. Kiss me—loved one—more—more! Your arms are like pale amber, your mouth blushes.... Waiter I asked for a plate of beef!"

The sun gleamed in through the window, and I could hear the horses below chewing oats. I sat and mumbled over my chip gaily, glad at heart as a child.

I kept all the time feeling for my manuscript. It wasn't really in my thoughts, but instinct told me it was there—'twas in my blood to remember it, and I took it out.

It had got wet, and I spread it out in the sun to dry; then I took to wandering up and down the room. How depressing everything looked! Small scraps of tin shavings were trodden into the floor; there was not a chair to sit upon, not even a nail in the bare walls. Everything had been brought to my "Uncle's," and consumed. A few sheets of paper lying on the table, covered with thick dust, were my sole possession; the old green blanket on the bed was lent to me by Hans Pauli some months ago.... Hans Pauli! I snap my fingers. Hans Pauli Pettersen shall help me! He would certainly be very angry that I had not appealed to him at once. I put on my hat in haste, gather up the manuscript, thrust it into my pocket, and hurry downstairs.

"Listen, Jens Olaj!" I called into the stable, "I am nearly certain I can help you in the afternoon."

Arrived at the Town Hall I saw that it was past eleven, and I determined on going to the editor at once. I stopped outside the office door to see if my sheets were paged rightly, smoothed them carefully out, put them back in my pocket, and knocked. My heart beat audibly as I entered.

"Scissors" is there as usual. I inquire timorously for the editor. No answer. The man sits and probes for minor items of news amongst the provincial papers.

I repeat my question, and advance a little farther.

"The editor has not come yet!" said "Scissors" at length, without looking up.

How soon would he come?

"Couldn't say—couldn't say at all!"

How long would the office be open?

To this I received no answer, so I was forced to leave. "Scissors" had not once looked up at me during all this scene; he had heard my voice, and recognized me by it. You are in such bad odour here, thought I, that he doesn't even take the trouble to answer you. I wonder if that is an order of the editor's. I had, 'tis true enough, right from the day my celebrated story was accepted for ten shillings, overwhelmed him with work, rushed to his door nearly every day with unsuitable things that he was obliged to peruse only to return them to me. Perhaps he wished to put an end to this—take stringent measures.... I took the road to Homandsbyen.

Hans Paul! Pettersen was a peasant-farmer's son, a student, living in the attic of a five-storied house; therefore, Hans Pauli Pettersen was a poor man. But if he had a shilling he wouldn't stint it. I would get it just as sure as if I already held it in my hand. And I rejoiced the whole time, as I went, over the shilling, and felt confident I would get it.

When I got to the street door it was closed and I had to ring.

"I want to see Student Pettersen," I said, and was about to step inside. "I know his room."

"Student Pettersen," repeats the girl. "Was it he who had the attic?" He had moved.

Well, she didn't know the address; but he had asked his letters to be sent to Hermansen in Tolbodgaden, and she mentioned the number.

I go, full of trust and hope, all the way to Tolbodgaden to ask Hans Pauli's address; being my last chance, I must turn it to account. On the way I came to a newly-built house, where a couple of joiners stood planing outside. I picked up a few satiny shavings from the heap, stuck one in my mouth, and the other in my pocket for by-and-by, and continued my journey.

I groaned with hunger. I had seen a marvellously large penny loaf at a baker's—the largest I could possibly get for the price.

"I come to find out Student Pettersen's address!"

"Bernt Akers Street, No. 10, in the attic." Was I going out there? Well, would I perhaps be kind enough to take out a couple of letters that had come for him?

I trudge up town again, along the same road, pass by the joiners—who are sitting with their cans between their knees, eating their good warm dinner from the Dampkökken—pass the bakers, where the loaf is still in its place, and at length reach Bernt Akers Street, half dead with fatigue. The door is open, and I mount all the weary stairs to the attic. I take the letters out of my pocket in order to put Hans Pauli into a good humour on the moment of my entrance.

He would be certain not to refuse to give me a helping hand when I explained how things were with me; no, certainly not; Hans Pauli had such a big heart—I had always said that of him.... I discovered his card fastened to the door—"H. P. Pettersen, Theological Student, 'gone home.'"

I sat down without more ado—sat down on the bare floor, dulled with fatigue, fairly beaten with exhaustion. I mechanically mutter, a couple of times, "Gone home—gone home!" then I keep perfectly quiet. There was not a tear in my eyes; I had not a thought, not a feeling of any kind. I sat and stared, with wide-open eyes, at the letters, without coming to any conclusion. Ten minutes went over—perhaps twenty or more. I sat stolidly on the one spot, and did not move a finger. This numb feeling of drowsiness was almost like a brief slumber. I hear some one come up the stairs.

"It was Student Pettersen, I ... I have two letters for him."

"He has gone home," replies the woman; "but he will return after the holidays. I could take the letters if you like!"

"Yes, thanks! that was all right," said I. "He could get them then when he came back; they might contain matters of importance. Good-morning."

When I got outside, I came to a standstill and said loudly in the open street, as I clenched my hands: "I will tell you one thing, my good Lord God, you are a bungler!" and I nod furiously, with set teeth, up to the clouds; "I will be hanged if you are not a bungler."

Then I took a few strides, and stopped again. Suddenly, changing my attitude, I fold my hands, hold my head to one side, and ask, with an unctuous, sanctimonious tone of voice: "Hast thou appealed also to him, my child?" It did not sound right!

With a large H, I say, with an H as big as a cathedral! once again, "Hast thou invoked Him, my child?" and I incline my head, and I make my voice whine, and answer, No!

That didn't sound right either.

You can't play the hypocrite, you idiot! Yes, you should say, I have invoked God my Father! and you must set your words to the most piteous tune you have ever heard in your life. So—o! Once again! Come, that was better! But you must sigh like a horse down with the colic. So—o! that's right. Thus I go, drilling myself in hypocrisy; stamp impatiently in the street when I fail to succeed; rail at myself for being such a blockhead, whilst the astonished passers-by turn round and stare at me.

I chewed uninterruptedly at my shaving, and proceeded, as steadily as I could, along the street. Before I realized it, I was at the railway square. The dock on Our Saviour's pointed to half-past one. I stood for a bit and considered. A faint sweat forced itself out on my face, and trickled down my eyelids. Accompany me down to the bridge, said I to myself—that is to say, if you have spare time!—and I made a bow to myself, and turned towards the railway bridge near the wharf.

The ships lay there, and the sea rocked in the sunshine. There was bustle and movement everywhere, shrieking steam-whistles, quay porters with cases on their shoulders, lively "shanties" coming from the prams. An old woman, a vendor of cakes, sits near me, and bends her brown nose down over her wares. The little table before her is sinfully full of nice things, and I turn away with distaste. She is filling the whole quay with her smell of cakes—phew! up with the windows!

I accosted a gentleman sitting at my side, and represented forcibly to him the nuisance of having cake-sellers here, cake-sellers there.... Eh? Yes; but he must really admit that.... But the good man smelt a rat, and did not give me time to finish speaking, for he got up and left. I rose, too, and followed him, firmly determined to convince him of his mistake.

"If it was only out of consideration for sanitary conditions," said I; and I slapped him on the shoulders.

"Excuse me, I am a stranger here, and know nothing of the sanitary conditions," he replied, and stared at me with positive fear.

Oh, that alters the case! if he was a stranger.... Could I not render him a service in any way? show him about? Really not? because it would be a pleasure to me, and it would cost him nothing....

But the man wanted absolutely to get rid of me, and he sheered off, in all haste, to the other side of the street.

I returned to the bench and sat down. I was fearfully disturbed, and the big street organ that had begun to grind a tune a little farther away made me still worse—a regular metallic music, a fragment of Weber, to which a little girl is singing a mournful strain. The flute-like sorrowfulness of the organ thrills through my blood; my nerves vibrate in responsive echo. A moment later, and I fall back on the seat, whimpering and crooning in time to it.

Oh, what strange freaks one's thoughts are guilty of when one is starving. I feel myself lifted up by these notes, dissolved in tones, and I float out, I feel so clearly. How I float out, soaring high above the mountains, dancing through zones of light!...

"A halfpenny," whines the little organ-girl, reaching forth her little tin plate; "only a halfpenny."

"Yes," I said, unthinkingly, and I sprang to my feet and ransacked all my pockets. But the child thinks I only want to make fun of her, and she goes away at once without saying a word.

This dumb forbearance was too much for me. If she had abused me, it would have been more endurable. I was stung with pain, and recalled her.

"I don't possess a farthing; but I will remember you later on, maybe tomorrow. What is your name? Yes, that is a pretty name; I won't forget it. Till tomorrow, then...."

But I understood quite well that she did not believe me, although she never said one word; and I cried with despair because this little street wench would not believe in me.

Once again I called her back, tore open my coat, and was about to give her my waistcoat. "I will make up to you for it," said I; "wait only a moment" ... and lo! I had no waistcoat.

What in the world made me look for it? Weeks had gone by since it was in my possession. What was the matter with me, anyway? The astonished child waited no longer, but withdrew fearsomely, and I was compelled to let her go. People throng round me, laugh aloud; a policeman thrusts his way through to me, and wants to know what is the row.

"Nothing!" I reply, "nothing at all; I only wanted to give the little girl over there my waistcoat ... for her father ... you needn't stand there and laugh at that ... I have only to go home and put on another."

"No disturbance in the street," says the constable; "so, march," and he gives me a shove on.

"Is them your papers?" he calls after me.

"Yes, by Jove! my newspaper leader; many important papers!

However could I be so careless?" I snatch up my manuscript, convince myself that it is lying in order and go, without stopping a second or looking about me, towards the editor's office.

It was now four by the clock of Our Saviour's Church. The office is shut. I stead noiselessly down the stairs, frightened as a thief, and stand irresolutely outside the door. What should I do now? I lean up against the wall, stare down at the stones, and consider. A pin is lying glistening at my feet; I stoop and pick it up. Supposing I were to cut the buttons off my coat, how much could I get for them? Perhaps it would be no use, though buttons are buttons; but yet, I look and examine them, and find them as good as new—that was a lucky idea all the same; I could cut them off with my penknife and take them to the pawn-office. The hope of being able to sell these five buttons cheered me immediately, and I cried, "See, see; it will all come right!" My delight got the upper hand of me, and I at once set to cut off the buttons one by one. Whilst thus occupied, I held the following hushed soliloquy:

Yes, you see one has become a little impoverished; a momentary embarrassment ... worn out, do you say? You must not make slips when you speak? I would like to see the person who wears out less buttons than I do, I can tell you! I always go with my coat open; it is a habit of mine, an idiosyncrasy.... No, no; of course, if you won't, well! But I must have a penny for them, at least.... No indeed! who said you were obliged to do it? You can hold your tongue, and leave me in peace.... Yes, well, you can fetch a policeman, can't you? I'll wait here whilst you are out looking for him, and I won't steal anything from you. Well, good-day! Good-day! My name, by the way, is Tangen; have been out a little late.

Some one comes up the stairs. I am recalled at once to reality. I recognize "Scissors," and put the buttons carefully into my pocket. He attempts to pass; doesn't even acknowledge my nod; is suddenly intently busied with his nails. I stop him, and inquire for the editor.

"Not in, do you hear."

"You lie," I said, and, with a cheek that fairly amazed myself, I continued, "I must have a word with him; it is a necessary errand—communications from the Stiftsgaarden.[5]

"Well, can't you tell me what it is, then?"

"Tell you?" and I looked "Scissors" up and down. This had the desired effect. He accompanied me at once, and opened the door. My heart was in my mouth now; I set my teeth, to try and revive my courage, knocked, and entered the editor's private office.

"Good-day! Is it you?" he asked kindly; "sit down."

If he had shown me the door it would have been almost as

---

[5] Dwelling of the civil governor of a Stift or diocese.

acceptable. I felt as if I were on the point of crying and said:

"I beg you will excuse...."

"Pray, sit down," he repeated. And I sat down, and explained that I again had an article which I was extremely anxious to get into his paper. I had taken such pains with it; it had cost me much effort.

"I will read it," said he, and he took it. "Everything you write is certain to cost you effort, but you are far too impetuous; if you could only be a little more sober. There's too much fever. In the meantime, I will read it," and he turned to the table again.

There I sat. Dared I ask for a shilling? explain to him why there was always fever? He would be sure to aid me; it was not the first time.

I stood up. Hum! But the last time I was with him he had complained about money, and had sent a messenger out to scrape some together for me. Maybe it might be the same case now. No; it should not occur! Could I not see then that he was sitting at work?

Was there otherwise anything? he inquired.

"No," I answered, and I compelled my voice to sound steady. "About how soon shall I call in again?"

"Oh, any time you are passing—in a couple of days or so."

I could not get my request over my lips. This man's friendliness seemed to me beyond bounds, and I ought to know how to appreciate it. Rather die of hunger! I went. Not even when I was outside the door, and felt once more the pangs of hunger, did I repent having left the office without having asked for that shilling. I took the other shaving out of my pocket and stuck it into my mouth. It helped. Why hadn't I done so before? "You ought to be ashamed of yourself," I said aloud. "Could it really have entered your head to ask the man for a shilling and put him to inconvenience again?" and I got downright angry with myself for the effrontery of which I had almost been guilty. "That is, by God! the shabbiest thing I ever heard," said I, "to rush at a man and nearly tear the eyes out of his head just because you happen to need a shilling, you miserable dog! So—o, march! quicker! quicker! you big thumping lout; I'll teach you." I commenced to run to punish myself, left one street after the other behind me at a bound, goaded myself on with suppressed cries, and shrieked dumbly and furiously at myself whenever I was about to halt. Thus I arrived a long way up Pyle Street, when at last I stood still, almost ready to cry with vexation at not being able to run any farther. I was trembling over my whole body, and I flung myself down on a step. "No; stop!" I said, and, in order to torture myself rightly, I arose again, and forced myself to keep standing. I jeered at myself and hugged myself with pleasure at the spectacle of my own exhaustion. At length, after the lapse of a few moments, I gave myself, with a nod, permission to be seated, though, even then, I chose the most uncomfortable place on the steps.

Lord! how delicious it was to rest! I dried the sweat off my face, and drew great refreshing breaths. How had I not run! But I was not sorry; I had richly deserved it. Why did I want to ask for that shilling? Now I could see the consequences, and I began to talk mildly to myself, dealing out admonitions as a mother might have done. I grew more and more moved, and tired and weak as I was, I fell a-crying. A quiet, heart-felt cry; an inner sobbing without a tear.

I sat for the space of a quarter of an hour, or more, in the same place. People came and went, and no one molested me. Little children played about around me, and a little bird sang on a tree on the other side of the street.

A policeman came towards me. "Why do you sit here?" said he.

"Why do I sit here?" I replied; "for pleasure."

"I have been watching you for the last half-hour. You've sat here now half-an-hour."

"About that," I replied; "anything more?"

I got up in a temper and walked on. Arrived at the market-place, I stopped and gazed down the street. For pleasure. Now, was that an answer to give? For weariness, you should have replied, and made your voice whining. You are a booby; you will never learn to dissemble. From exhaustion, and you should have gasped like a horse.

When I got to the fire look-out, I halted afresh, seized by a new idea. I snapped my fingers, burst into a loud laugh that confounded the passers-by, and said: "Now you shall just go to Levion the parson. You shall, as sure as death—ay, just for a try. What have you got to lose by it? and it is such glorious weather!"

I entered Pascha's book-shop, found Pastor Levion's address in the directory, and started for it.

Now for it! said I. Play no pranks. Conscience, did you say? No rubbish, if you please. You are too poor to support a conscience. You are hungry; you have come on important business—the first thing needful. But you shall hold your head askew, and set your words to a sing-song. You won't! What? Well then, I won't go a step farther. Do you hear that? Indeed, you are in a sorely tempted condition, fighting with the powers of darkness and great voiceless monsters at night, so that it is a horror to think of; you hunger and thirst for wine and milk, and don't get them. It has gone so far with you. Here you stand and haven't as much as a halfpenny to bless yourself with. But you believe in grace, the Lord be praised; you haven't yet lost your faith; and then you must clasp your hands together, and look a very Satan of a fellow for believing in grace. As far as Mammon was concerned, why, you hated Mammon with all its pomps in any form. Now it's quite another thing with a psalm-book—a souvenir to the extent of a few shillings.... I stopped at the pastor's door, and read, "Office hours, 12 to 4."

Mind, no fudge, I said; now we'll go ahead in earnest! So hang your head a little more, and I rang at the private entrance.

"I want to see the pastor," said I to the maid; but it was not possible for me to get in God's name yet awhile.

"He has gone out."

Gone out, gone out! That destroyed my whole plan; scattered all I intended to say to the four winds. What had I gained then by the long walk? There I stood.

"Was it anything particular?" questioned the maid.

"Not at all," I replied, "not at all." It was only just that it was such glorious God's weather that I thought I would come out and make a call.

There I stood, and there she stood. I purposely thrust out my chest to attract her attention to the pin that held my coat together. I implored her with a look to see what I had come for, but the poor creature didn't understand it at all.

Lovely God's weather. Was not the mistress at home either?

Yes; but she had gout, and lay on a sofa without being able to move herself.... Perhaps I would leave a message or something?

No, not at all; I only just took walks like this now and again, just for exercise; it was so wholesome after dinner.... I set out on the road back—what would gossiping longer lead to? Besides, I commenced to feel dizzy. There was no mistake about it; I was about to break down in earnest. Office hours from 12 to 4. I had knocked at the door an hour too late. The time of grace was over. I sat down on one of the benches near the church in the market. Lord! how black things began to look for me now! I did not cry; I was too utterly tired, worn to the last degree. I sat there without trying to arrive at any conclusion, sad, motionless, and starving. My chest was much inflamed; it smarted most strangely and sorely—nor would chewing shavings help me much longer. My jaws were tired of that barren work, and I let them rest. I simply gave up. A brown orange-peel, too, I had found in the street, and which I had at once commenced to chew, had given me nausea. I was ill—the veins swelled up bluely on my wrists. What was it I had really sought after? Run about the whole live-long day for a shilling, that would but keep life in me for a few hours longer. Considering all, was it not a matter of indifference if the inevitable took place one day earlier or one day later? If I had conducted myself like an ordinary being I should have gone home long ago, and laid myself down to rest, and given in. My mind was clear for a moment. Now I was to die. It was in the time of the fall, and all things were hushed to sleep. I had tried every means, exhausted every resource of which I knew. I fondled this thought sentimentally, and each time I still hoped for a possible succour I whispered repudiatingly: "You fool, you have already begun to die."

I ought to write a couple of letters, make all ready—prepare myself. I would wash myself carefully and tidy my bed nicely. I would lay my head upon the sheets of white paper, the cleanest things I had left, and the green blanket. I ... The green blanket! Like a shot I was wide awake. The blood mounted to my head, and I got violent palpitation of the heart. I arise from the seat, and start to walk. Life stirs again in all my fibres, and time after time I repeat disconnectedly, "The green blanket—the green blanket." I go faster and faster, as if it is a case of fetching something, and stand after a little time in my tinker's workshop. Without pausing a moment, or wavering in my resolution, I go over to the bed, and roll up Hans Pauli's blanket. It was a strange thing if this bright idea of mine couldn't save me. I rose infinitely superior to the stupid scruples which sprang up in me—half inward cries about a certain stain on my honour. I bade good-bye to the whole of them. I was no hero—no virtuous idiot. I had my senses left.

So I took the blanket under my arm and went to No. 5 Stener's Street. I knocked, and entered the big, strange room for the first time. The bell on the door above my head gave a lot of violent jerks. A man enters from a side room, chewing, his mouth is full of food, and stands behind the counter.

"Eh, lend me sixpence on my eye-glasses?" said I. "I shall release them in a couple of days, without fail—eh?"

"No! they're steel, aren't they?"

"Yes."

"No; can't do it."

"Ah, no, I suppose you can't. Well, it was really at best only a joke. Well, I have a blanket with me for which, properly speaking, I have no longer any use, and it struck me that you might take it off my hands."

"I have—more's the pity—a whole store full of bed-clothes," he replied; and when I had opened it he just cast one glance over it and said, "No, excuse me, but I haven't any use for that either."

"I wanted to show you the worse side first," said I; "it's much better on the other side."

"Ay, ay; it's no good. I won't own it; and you wouldn't raise a penny on it anywhere."

"No, it's clear it isn't worth anything," I said; "but I thought it might go with another old blanket at an auction."

"Well, no; it's no use."

"Three pence?" said I.

"No; I won't have it at all, man! I wouldn't have it in the house!" I took it under my arm and went home.

I acted as if nothing had passed, spread it over the bed again, smoothed it well out, as was my custom, and tried to wipe away every trace of my late action. I could not possibly have been in my right mind at the moment when I came to the conclusion to commit this rascally trick. The more I thought over it the more unreasonable it seemed to me. It must have been an attack of weakness; some relaxation in my inner self that had surprised me when off my guard. Neither had I fallen straight into the trap. I had half felt that I was going the wrong road, and I expressly offered my glasses first, and I rejoiced greatly that I had not had the opportunity of carrying into effect this fault which would have sullied the last hours I had to live.

I wandered out into the city again. I let myself sink upon one of the seats by Our Saviour's Church; dozed with my head on my breast, apathetic after my last excitement, sick and famished with hunger. And time went by.

I should have to sit out this hour, too. It was a little lighter outside than in the house, and it seemed to me that my chest did not pain quite so badly out in the open air. I should get home, too, soon enough—and I dozed, and thought, and suffered fearfully.

I had found a little pebble; I wiped it clean on my coat sleeve and put it into my mouth so that I might have something to mumble. Otherwise I did not stir, and didn't even wink an eyelid. People came and went; the noise of cars, the tramp of hoofs, and chatter of tongues filled the air. I might try with the buttons. Of course there would be no use in trying; and besides, I was now in a rather bad way; but when I came to consider the matter closely, I would be obliged, as it were, to pass in the direction of my "Uncle's" as I went home. At last I got up, dragging myself slowly to my feet, and reeled down the streets. It began to burn over my eyebrows—fever was setting in, and I hurried as fast as I could. Once more I passed the baker's shop where the little loaf lay. "Well, we must stop here!" I said, with affected decision. But supposing I were to go in and beg for a bit of bread? Surely that was a fleeting thought, a flash; it could never really have occurred to me seriously. "Fie!" I whispered to myself, and shook my head, and held on my way. In Rebslager a pair of lovers stood in a doorway and talked together softly; a little farther up a girl popped her head out of a window. I walked so slowly and thoughtfully, that I looked as if I might be deep in meditation on nothing in particular, and the wench came out into the street. "How is the world treating you, old fellow? Eh, what, are you ill? Nay, the Lord preserve us, what a face!" and she drew away frightened. I pulled up at once: What's amiss with my face? Had I really begun to die? I felt over my cheeks with my hand; thin—naturally, I was thin—my cheeks were like two hollowed bowls; but Lord ... I reeled along again, but again came to a standstill; I must be quite inconceivably thin. Who knows but that my eyes were sinking right into my head? How did I look in reality? It was the very deuce that one must let oneself turn into a living deformity for sheer hunger's sake. Once more I was seized by fury, a last flaring up, a final spasm. "Preserve me, what a face. Eh?" Here I was, with a head that couldn't be matched in the whole country, with a pair of fists that, by the Lord, could grind a navvy into finest dust, and yet I went and hungered myself into a deformity, right in the town of Christiania. Was there any rhyme or reason in that? I had sat in saddle, toiled day and night like a carrier's horse.

I had read my eyes out of their sockets, had starved the brains out of my head, and what the devil had I gained by it? Even a street hussy prayed God to deliver her from the sight of me. Well, now, there should be a stop to it. Do you understand that? Stop it shall, or the devil take a worse hold of me.

With steadily increasing fury, grinding my teeth under the consciousness of my impotence, with tears and oaths I raged on, without looking at the people who passed me by. I commenced once more to martyr myself, ran my forehead against lamp-posts on purpose, dug my nails deep into my palms, bit my tongue with frenzy when it didn't articulate clearly, and laughed insanely each time it hurt much.

Yes; but what shall I do? I asked myself at last, and I stamped many times on the pavement and repeated, What shall I do? A gentleman just going by remarks, with a smile, "You ought to go and ask to be locked up." I looked after him. One of our well-known lady's doctors, nicknamed "The Duke." Not even he understood my real condition—a man I knew; whose hand I had shaken. I grew quiet. Locked up? Yes, I was mad; he was right. I felt madness in my blood; felt its darting pain through my brain. So that was to be the end of me! Yes, yes; and I resume my wearisome, painful walk. There was the haven in which I was to find rest.

Suddenly I stop again. But not locked up! I say, not that; and I grew almost hoarse with fear. I implored grace for myself; begged to the wind and weather not to be locked up. I should have to be brought to the guard-house again, imprisoned in a dark cell which had not a spark of light in it. Not that! There must be other channels yet open that I had not tried, and I would try them. I would be so earnestly painstaking; would take good time for it, and go indefatigably round from house to house. For example, there was Cisler the music-seller; I hadn't been to him at all. Some remedy would turn up!.... Thus I stumbled on, and talked until I brought myself to weep with emotion. Cisler! Was that perchance a hint from on high? His name had struck me for no reason, and he lived so far away; but I would look him up all the same, go slowly, and rest between times. I knew the place well; I had been there often, when times were good had bought much music from him. Should I ask him for sixpence? Perhaps that might make him feel uncomfortable. I would ask him for a shilling. I went into the shop, and asked for the chief. They showed me into his office; there he sat—handsome, well-dressed in the latest style—running down some accounts. I stammered through an excuse, and set forth my errand. Compelled by need to apply to him ... it should not be very long till I could pay it back ... when I got paid for my newspaper article.... He would confer such a great benefit on me.... Even as I was speaking he turned about to his desk, and resumed his work. When I had finished, he glanced sideways at me, shook his handsome head, and said, "No"; simply "no"—no explanation—not another word.

My knees trembled fearfully, and I supported myself against the little polished barrier. I must try once more. Why should just his name have occurred to me as I stood far away from there in "It won't be I that will do that," he observed; adding, "and let me tell you, at the same time, I've had about enough of this."

I tore myself out, sick with hunger, and boiling with shame. I had turned myself into a dog for the sake of a miserable bone, and I had not got it. Nay, now there must be an end of this! It had really gone all too far with me. I had held myself up for many years, stood erect through so many hard hours, and now, all at once, I had sunk to the lowest form of begging. This one day had coarsened my whole mind, bespattered my soul with shamelessness. I had not been too abashed to stand and whine in the pettiest huckster's shop, and what had it availed me?

But was I not then without the veriest atom of bread to put inside my mouth? I had succeeded in rendering myself a thing loathsome to myself. Yes, yes; but it must come to an end. Presently they would lock the outer door at home? I must hurry unless I wished to lie in the guard-house again.

This gave me strength. Lie in that cell again I would not. With body bent forward, and my hands pressed hard against my left ribs to deaden the stings a little, I struggled on, keeping my eyes fastened upon the paving-stones that I might not be forced to bow to possible acquaintances, and hastened to the fire look-out. God be praised! it was only seven o'clock by the dial on Our Saviour's; I had three hours yet before the door would be locked. What a fright I had been in!

Well, there was not a stone left unturned. I had done all I could. To think that I really could not succeed once in a whole day! If I told it no one could believe it; if I were to write it down they would say I had invented it. Not in a single place! Well, well, there is no help for it. Before all, don't go and get pathetic again. Bah! how disgusting! I can assure you, it makes me have a loathing for you. If all hope is over, why there is an end of it. Couldn't I, for that matter, steal a handful of oats in the stable? A streak of light—a ray—yet I knew the stable was shut.

I took my ease, and crept home at a slow snail's pace. I felt thirsty, luckily for the first time through the whole day, and I went and sought about for a place where I could get a drink. I was a long distance away from the bazaar, and I would not ask at a private house. Perhaps, though, I could wait till I got home; it would take a quarter of an hour. It was not at all so certain that I could keep down a draught of water, either; my stomach no longer suffered in any way—I even felt nausea at the spittle I swallowed. But the buttons! I had not tried the buttons at all yet. There I stood, stock-still, and commenced to smile. Maybe there was a remedy, in spite of all! I wasn't totally doomed. I should certainly get a penny for them; tomorrow I might raise another some place or other, and Thursday I might be paid for my newspaper article. I should just see it would come out all right. To think that I could really go and forget the buttons. I took them out of my pocket, and inspected them as I walked on again. My eyes grew dazed with joy. I did not see the street; I simply went on. Didn't I know exactly the big pawn-shop—my refuge in the dark evenings, with my blood-sucking friend? One by one my possessions had vanished there—my little things from home—my last book. I liked to go there on auction days, to look on, and rejoice each time my books seemed likely to fall into good hands. Magelsen, the actor, had my watch; I was almost proud of that. A diary, in which I had written my first small poetical attempt, had been bought by an acquaintance, and my topcoat had found a haven with a photographer, to be used in the studio. So there was no cause to grumble about any of them. I held my buttons ready in my hand; "Uncle" is sitting at his desk, writing. "I am not in a hurry," I say, afraid of disturbing him, and making him impatient at my application. My voice sounded so curiously hollow I hardly recognized it again, and my heart beat like a sledge-hammer.

He came smilingly over to me, as was his wont, laid both his hands flat on the counter, and looked at my face without saying anything. Yes, I had brought something of which I would ask him if he could make any use; something which is only in my way at home, assure you of it—are quite an annoyance—some buttons. Well, what then? what was there about the buttons? and he thrusts his eyes down close to my hand. Couldn't he give me a couple of halfpence for them?—whatever he thought himself—quite according to his own judgment. "For the buttons?"—and "Uncle" stares astonishedly at me—"for these buttons?" Only for a cigar or whatever he liked himself; I was just passing, and thought I would look in.

Upon this, the old pawnbroker burst out laughing, and returned to his desk without saying a word. There I stood; I had not hoped for much, yet, all the same, I had thought of a possibility of being helped. This laughter was my death-warrant. It couldn't, I suppose, be of any use trying with my eyeglasses either? Of course, I would let my glasses go in with them; that was a matter of course, said I, and I took them off. Only a penny, or if he wished, a halfpenny.

"You know quite well I can't lend you anything on your glasses," said "Uncle"; I told you that once before."

"But I want a stamp," I said, dully. "I can't even send off the letters I have written; a penny or a halfpenny stamp, just as you will."

"Oh, God help you, go your way!" he replied, and motioned me off with his hands.

Yes, yes; well, it must be so, I said to myself. Mechanically, I put on my glasses again, took the buttons in my hand, and, turning away, bade him good-night, and closed the door after me as usual. Well, now, there was nothing more to be done! To think he would not take them at any price, I muttered. They are almost new buttons; I can't understand it.

Whilst I stood, lost in thought, a man passed by and entered the office. He had given me a little shove in his hurry. We both made excuses, and I turned round and looked after him.

"What! is that you?" he said, suddenly, when half-way up the steps. He came back, and I recognized him. "God bless me, man, what on earth do you look like? What were you doing in there?"

"Oh, I had business. You are going in too, I see."

"Yes; what were you in with?"

My knees trembled; I supported myself against the wall, and stretched out my hand with the buttons in it.

"What the deuce!" he cried. "No; this is really going too far."

"Good-night!" said I, and was about to go; I felt the tears choking my breast.

"No; wait a minute," he said.

What was I to wait for? Was he not himself on the road to my "Uncle," bringing, perhaps, his engagement ring—had been hungry, perhaps, for several days—owed his landlady?

"Yes," I replied; "if you will be out soon...."

"Of course," he broke in, seizing hold of my arm; "but I may as well tell you I don't believe you. You are such an idiot, that it's better you come in along with me."

I understood what he meant, suddenly felt a little spark of pride, and answered:

"I can't; I promised to be in Bernt Akers Street at half-past seven, and...."

"Half-past seven, quite so; but it's eight now. Here I am, standing with the watch in my hand that I'm going to pawn. So, in with you, you hungry sinner! I'll get you five shillings anyhow," and he pushed me in.

Part III

A week passed in glory and gladness.

I had got over the worst this time, too. I had had food every day, and my courage rose, and I thrust one iron after the other into the fire.

I was working at three or four articles, that plundered my poor brain of every spark, every thought that rose in it; and yet I fancied that I wrote with more facility than before.

The last article with which I had raced about so much, and upon which I had built such hopes, had already been returned to me by the editor; and, angry and wounded as I was, I had destroyed it immediately, without even re-reading it again. In future, I would try another paper in order to open up more fields for my work.

Supposing that writing were to fail, and the worst were to come to the worst, I still had the ships to take to. The Nun lay alongside the wharf, ready to sail, and I might, perhaps, work my way out to Archangel, or wherever else she might be bound; there was no lack of openings on many sides. The last crisis had dealt rather roughly with me. My hair fell out in masses, and I was much troubled with headaches, particularly in the morning, and my nervousness died a hard death. I sat and wrote during the day with my hands bound up in rags, simply because I could not endure the touch of my own breath upon them. If Jens Olaj banged the stable door underneath me, or if a dog came into the yard and commenced to bark, it thrilled through my very marrow like icy stabs piercing me from every side. I was pretty well played out.

Day after day I strove at my work, begrudging myself the short time it took to swallow my food before I sat down again to write. At this time both the bed and the little rickety table were strewn over with notes and written pages, upon which I worked turn about, added any new ideas which might have occurred to me during the day, erased, or quickened here and there the dull points by a word of colour—fagged and toiled at sentence after sentence, with the greatest of pains. One afternoon, one of my articles being at length finished, I thrust it, contented and happy, into my pocket, and betook myself to the "Commodore." It was high time I made some arrangement towards getting a little money again; I had only a few pence left.

The " Commodore" requested me to sit down for a moment; he would be disengaged immediately, and he continued writing.

I looked about the little office—busts, prints, cuttings, and an enormous paper-basket, that looked as if it might swallow a man, bones and all. I felt sad at heart at the sight of this monstrous chasm, this dragon's mouth, that always stood open, always ready to receive rejected work, newly crushed hopes.

"What day of the month is it?" queried the " Commodore" from the table.

"The 28th," I reply, pleased that I can be of service to him, "the 28th," and he continues writing. At last he encloses a couple of letters in their envelopes, tosses some papers into the basket, and lays down his pen. Then he swings round on his chair, and looks at me. Observing that I am still standing near the door, he makes a half-serious, half-playful motion with his hand, and points to a chair.

I turn aside, so that he may not see that I have no waistcoat on, when I open my coat to take the manuscript out of my pocket.

"It is only a little character sketch of Correggio," I say; "but perhaps it is, worse luck, not written in such a way that...."

He takes the papers out of my hand, and commences to go through them. His face is turned towards me.

And so it is thus he looks at close quarters, this man, whose name I had already heard in my earliest youth, and whose paper had exercised the greatest influence upon me as the years advanced? His hair is curly, and his beautiful brown eyes are a little restless. He has a habit of tweaking his nose now and then. No Scotch minister could look milder than this truculent writer, whose pen always left bleeding scars wherever it attacked. A peculiar feeling of awe and admiration comes over me in the presence of this man. The tears are on the point of coming to my eyes, and I advanced a step to tell him how heartily I appreciated him, for all he had taught me, and to beg him not to hurt me; I was only a poor bungling wretch, who had had a sorry enough time of it as it was....

He looked up, and placed my manuscript slowly together, whilst he sat and considered. To make it easier for him to give me a refusal, I stretch out my hand a little, and say:

"Ah, well, of course, it is not of any use to you," and I smile to give him the impression that I take it easily.

"Everything has to be of such a popular nature to be of any use to us," he replies; "you know the kind of public we have. But can't you try and write something a little more commonplace, or hit upon something that people understand better?"

His forbearance astonishes me. I understand that my article is rejected, and yet I could not have received a prettier refusal. Not to take up his time any longer, I reply:

"Oh yes, I daresay I can."

I go towards the door. Hem—he must pray forgive me for having taken up his time with this ... I bow, and turn the door handle.

"If you need it," he says, "you are welcome to draw a little in advance; you can write for it, you know."

Now, as he had just seen that I was not capable of writing, this offer humiliated me somewhat, and I answered:

"No, thanks; I can pull through yet a while, thanking you very much, all the same. Good-day!"

"Good-day!" replies the "Commodore," turning at the same time to his desk again.

He had none the less treated me with undeserved kindness, and I was grateful to him for it—and I would know how to appreciate it too. I made a resolution not to return to him until I could take something with me, that satisfied me perfectly; something that would astonish the "Commodore " a bit, and make him order me to be paid half-a-sovereign without a moment's hesitation. I went home, and tackled my writing once more.

During the following evenings, as soon as it got near eight o'clock and the gas was lit, the following thing happened regularly to me.

As I come out of my room to take a walk in the streets after the labour and troubles of the day, a lady, dressed in black, stands under the lamp-post exactly opposite my door.

She turns her face towards me and follows me with her eyes when I pass her by—I remark that she always has the same dress on, always the same thick veil that conceals her face and falls over her breast, and that she carries in her hand a small umbrella with an ivory ring in the handle. This was already the third evening I had seen her there, always in the same place. As soon as I have passed her by she turns slowly and goes down the street away from me. My nervous brain vibrated with curiosity, and I became at once possessed by the unreasonable feeling that I was the object of her visit. At last I was almost on the point of addressing her, of asking her if she was looking for any one, if she needed my assistance in any way, or if I might accompany her home. Badly dressed, as I unfortunately was, I might protect her through the dark streets; but I had an undefined fear that it perhaps might cost me something; a glass of wine, or a drive, and I had no money left at all. My distressingly empty pockets acted in a far too depressing way upon me, and I had not even the courage to scrutinize her sharply as I passed her by. Hunger had once more taken up its abode in my breast, and I had not tasted food since yesterday evening. This, 'tis true, was not a long period; I had often been able to hold out for a couple of days at a time, but latterly I had commenced to fall off seriously; I could not go hungry one quarter as well as I used to do. A single day made me feel dazed, and I suffered from perpetual retching the moment I tasted water. Added to this was the fact that I lay and shivered all night, lay fully dressed as I stood and walked in the daytime, lay blue with cold, lay and froze every night with fits of icy shivering, and grew stiff during my sleep. The old blanket could not keep out the draughts, and I woke in the mornings with my nose stopped by the sharp outside frosty air which forced its way into the dilapidated room.

I go down the street and think over what I am to do to keep myself alive until I get my next article finished. If I only had a candle I would try to fag on through the night; it would only take a couple of hours if I once warmed to my work, and then tomorrow I could call on the "Commodore."

I go without further ado into the Opland Cafe and look for my young acquaintance in the bank, in order to procure a penny for a candle. I passed unhindered through all the rooms; I passed a dozen tables at which men sat chatting, eating, and drinking; I passed into the back of the cafe, ay, even into the red alcove, without succeeding in finding my man.

Crestfallen and annoyed I dragged myself out again into the street and took the direction to the Palace.

Wasn't it now the very hottest eternal devil existing to think that my hardships never would come to an end! Taking long, furious strides, with the collar of my coat hunched savagely up round my ears, and my hands thrust in my breeches pockets, I strode along, cursing my unlucky stars the whole way. Not one real untroubled hour in seven or eight months, not the common food necessary to hold body and soul together for the space of one short week, before want stared me in the face again. Here I had, into the bargain, gone and kept straight and honourable all through my misery—Ha! ha! straight and honourable to the heart's core. God preserve me, what a fool I had been! And I commenced to tell myself how I had even gone about conscience-stricken because I had once brought Hans Pauli's blanket to the pawn-broker's. I laughed sarcastically at my delicate rectitude, spat contemptuously in the street, and could not find words half strong enough to mock myself for my stupidity. Let it only happen now! Were I to find at this moment a schoolgirl's savings or a poor widow's only penny, I would snatch it up and pocket it; steal it deliberately, and sleep the whole night through like a top. I had not suffered so unspeakably much for nothing—my patience was gone—I was prepared to do anything.

I walked round the palace three, perhaps four, times, then came to the conclusion that I would go home, took yet one little turn in the park and went back down Carl Johann. It was now about eleven. The streets were fairly dark, and the people roamed about in all directions, quiet pairs and noisy groups mixed with one another. The great hour had commenced, the pairing time when the mystic traffic is in full swing—and the hour of merry adventures sets in. Rustling petticoats, one or two still short, sensual laughter, heaving bosoms, passionate, panting breaths, and far down near the Grand Hotel, a voice calling "Emma!" The whole street was a swamp, from which hot vapours exuded.

I feel involuntarily in my pockets for a few shillings. The passion that thrills through the movements of every one of the passers-by, the dim light of the gas lamps, the quiet pregnant night, all commence to affect me—this air, that is laden with whispers, embraces, trembling admissions, concessions, half-uttered words and suppressed cries. A number of cats are declaring their love with loud yells in Blomquist's doorway. And I did not possess even a florin! It was a misery, a wretchedness without parallel to be so impoverished. What humiliation, too; what disgrace! I began again to think about the poor widow's last mite, that I would have stolen a schoolboy's cap or handkerchief, or a beggar's wallet, that I would have brought to a rag-dealer without more ado, and caroused with the proceeds.

In order to console myself—to indemnify myself in some measure—I take to picking all possible faults in the people who glide by. I shrug my shoulders contemptuously, and look slightingly at them according as they pass. These easily-pleased, confectionery-eating students, who fancy they are sowing their wild oats in truly Continental style if they tickle a sempstress under the ribs! These young bucks, bank clerks, merchants, flâneurs—who would not disdain a sailor's wife; blowsy Molls, ready to fall down in the first doorway for a glass of beer! What sirens! The place at their side still warm from the last night's embrace of a watch-man or a stable-boy! The throne always vacant, always open to newcomers! Pray, mount!

I spat out over the pavement, without troubling if it hit any one. I felt enraged; filled with contempt for these people who scraped acquaintanceship with one another, and paired off right before my eyes. I lifted my head, and felt in myself the blessing of being able to keep my own sty clean. At Stortingsplads (Parliament Place) I met a girl who looked fixedly at me as I came close to her.

"Good-night!" said I.

"Good-night!" She stopped.

Hum! was she out walking so late? Did not a young lady run rather a risk in being in Carl Johann at this time of night? Really not? Yes; but was she never spoken to, molested, I meant; to speak plainly, asked to go along home with any one?

She stared at me with astonishment, scanned my face closely, to see what I really meant by this, then thrust her hand suddenly under my arm, and said:

"Yes, and we went too!"

I walked on with her. But when we had gone a few paces past the car-stand I came to a standstill, freed my arm, and said:

"Listen, my dear, I don't own a farthing!" and with that I went on.

At first she would not believe me; but after she had searched all my pockets, and found nothing, she got vexed, tossed her head, and called me a dry cod.

"Good-night!" said I.

"Wait a minute," she called; "are those eyeglasses that you've got gold?"

"No."

"Then go to blazes with you!" and I went.

A few seconds after she came running behind me, and called out to me:

"You can come with me all the same!"

I felt humiliated by this offer from an unfortunate street wench, and I said "No." Besides, it was growing late at night, and I was due at a place. Neither could she afford to make sacrifices of that kind.

"Yes; but now I will have you come with me."

"But I won't go with you in this way."

"Oh, naturally; you are going with some one else."

"No," I answered.

But I was conscious that I stood in a sorry plight in face of this unique street jade, and I made up my mind to save appearances at least.

"What is your name?" I inquired. "Mary, eh? Well, listen to me now, Mary!" and I set about explaining my behaviour. The girl grew more and more astonished in measure as I proceeded. Had she then believed that I, too, was one of those who went about the street at night and ran after little girls? Did she really think so badly of me? Had I perhaps said anything rude to her from the beginning? Did one behave as I had done when one was actuated by any bad motive? Briefly, in so many words, I had accosted her, and accompanied her those few paces, to see how far she would go on with it. For the rest, my name was So-and-so—Pastor So-and-so. "Good-night; depart, and sin no more!" With these words I left her.

I rubbed my hands with delight over my happy notion, and soliloquized aloud, "What a joy there is in going about doing good actions." Perhaps I had given this fallen creature an upward impulse for her whole life; save her, once for all, from destruction, and she would appreciate it when she came to think over it; remember me yet in her hour of death with thankful heart. Ah! in truth, it paid to be honourable, upright, and righteous!

My spirits were effervescing. I felt fresh and courageous enough to face anything that might turn up. If I only had a candle, I might perhaps complete my article. I walked on, jingling my new door-key in my hand; hummed, and whistled, and speculated as to means of procuring a candle. There was no other way out of it. I would have to take my writing materials with me into the street, under a lamp-post. I opened the door, and went up to get my papers. When I descended once more I locked the door from the outside, and planted myself under the light. All around was quiet; I heard the heavy clanking footstep of a constable down in Tærgade, and far away in the direction of St. Han's Hill a dog barked. There was nothing to disturb me. I pulled my coat collar up round my ears, and commenced to think with all my might.

It would be such an extraordinary help to me if I were lucky enough to find a suitable winding up for this little essay. I had stuck just at a rather difficult point in it, where there ought to be a quite imperceptible transition to something fresh, then a subdued gliding finale, a prolonged murmur, ending at last in a climax as bold and as startling as a shot, or the sound of a mountain avalanche—full stop. But the words would not come to me. I read over the whole piece from the commencement; read every sentence aloud, and yet failed absolutely to crystallize my thoughts, in order to produce this scintillating climax. And into the bargain, whilst I was standing labouring away at this, the constable came and, planting himself a little distance away from me, spoilt my whole mood. Now, what concern was it of his if I stood and strove for a striking climax to an article for the Commodore? Lord, how utterly impossible it was for me to keep my head above water, no matter how much I tried! I stayed there for the space of an hour. The constable went his way. The cold began to get too intense for me to keep still. Disheartened and despondent over this abortive effort, I opened the door again, and went up to my room.

It was cold up there, and I could barely see my window for the intense darkness. I felt my towards the bed, pulled off my shoes, and set about warming my feet between my hands. Then I lay down, as I had done for a long time now, with all my clothes on.

The following morning I sat up in bed as soon as it got light, and set to work at the essay once more. I sat thus till noon; I had succeeded by then in getting ten, perhaps twenty lines down, and still I had not found an ending.

I rose, put on my shoes, and began to walk up and down the floor to try and warm myself. I looked out; there was rime on the window; it was snowing. Down in the yard a thick layer of snow covered the paving-stones and the top of the pump. I bustled about the room, took aimless turns to and fro, scratched the wall with my nail, leant my head carefully against the door for a while, tapped with my forefinger on the floor, and then listened attentively, all without any object, but quietly and pensively as if it were some matter of importance in which I was engaged; and all the while I murmured aloud, time upon time, so that I could hear my own voice.

But, great God, surely this is madness! and yet I kept on just as before. After a long time, perhaps a couple of hours, I pulled myself sharply together, bit my lips, and manned myself as well as I could. There must be an end to this! I found a splinter to chew, and set myself resolutely to again.

A couple of short sentences formed themselves with much trouble, a score of poor words which I tortured forth with might and main to try and advance a little. Then I stopped, my head was barren; I was incapable of more. And, as I could positively not go on, I set myself to gaze with wide open eyes at these last words, this unfinished sheet of paper; I stared at these strange, shaky letters that bristled up from the paper like small hairy creeping things, till at last I could neither make head nor tail of any of it. I thought on nothing.

Time went; I heard the traffic in the street, the rattle of cars and tramp of hoofs. Jens Olaj's voice ascended towards me from the stables as he chid the horses. I was perfectly stunned. I sat and moistened my lips a little, but otherwise made no effort to do anything; my chest was in a pitiful state. The dusk closed in; I sank more and more together, grew weary, and lay down on the bed again. In order to warm my fingers a little I stroked them through my hair backwards and forwards and crosswise. Small loose tufts came away, flakes that got between my fingers, and scattered over the pillow. I did not think anything about it just then; it was as if it did not concern me. I had hair enough left, anyway. I tried afresh to shake myself out of this strange daze that enveloped my whole being like a mist. I sat up, struck my knees with my flat hands, laughed as hard as my sore chest permitted me—only to collapse again. Naught availed; I was dying helplessly, with my eyes wide open—staring straight up at the roof. At length I stuck my forefinger in my mouth, and took to sucking it. Something stirred in my brain, a thought that bored its way in there—a stark-mad notion.

Supposing I were to take a bite? And without a moment's reflection, I shut my eyes, and clenched my teeth on it.

I sprang up. At last I was thoroughly awake. A little blood trickled from it, and I licked it as it came. It didn't hurt very much, neither was the wound large, but I was brought at one bound to my senses. I shook my head, went to the window, where I found a rag, and wound it round the sore place. As I stood and busied myself with this, my eyes filled with tears; I cried softly to myself. This poor thin finger looked so utterly pitiable. God in Heaven! what a pass it had come to now with me! The gloom grew closer. It was, maybe, not impossible that I might work up my finale through the course of the evening, if I only had a candle. My head was clear once more. Thoughts came and went as usual, and I did not suffer particularly; I did not even feel hunger so badly as some hours previously. I could hold out well till the next day. Perhaps I might be able to get a candle on credit, if I applied to the provision shop and explained my situation—I was so well known in there; in the good old days, when I had the means to do it, I used to buy many a loaf there. There was no doubt I could raise a candle on the strength of my honest name; and for the first time for ages I took to brushing my clothes a little, got rid as well as the darkness allowed me of the loose hairs on my collar, and felt my way down the stairs.

When I got outside in the street it occurred to me that I might perhaps rather ask for a loaf. I grew irresolute, and stopped to consider. "On no account," I replied to myself at last; I was unfortunately not in a condition to bear food. It would only be a repetition of the same old story—visions, and presentiments, and mad notions. My article would never get finished, and it was a question of going to the "Commodore" before he had time to forget me. On no account whatever! and I decided upon the candle. With that I entered the shop.

A woman is standing at the counter making purchases; several small parcels in different sorts of paper are lying in front of her. The shopman, who knows me, and knows what I usually buy, leaves the woman, and packs without much ado a loaf in a piece of paper and shoves it over to me.

"No, thank you, it was really a candle I wanted this evening," I say. I say it very quietly and humbly, in order not to vex him and spoil my chance of getting what I want.

My answer confuses him; he turns quite cross at my unexpected words; it was the first time I had ever demanded anything but a loaf from him.

"Well then, you must wait a while," he says at last, and busies himself with the woman's parcels again.

She receives her wares and pays for them—-gives him a florin, out of which she gets the change, and goes out. Now the shop-boy and I are alone. He says:

"So it was a candle you wanted, eh?" He tears open a package, and takes one out for me. He looks at me, and I look at him; I can't get my request over my lips.

"Oh yes, that's true; you paid, though!" he says suddenly. He simply asserts that I had paid. I heard every word, and he begins to count some silver out of the till, coin after coin, shining stout pieces. He gives me back change for a crown.

"Much obliged," he says.

Now I stand and look at these pieces of money for a second. I am conscious something is wrong somewhere. I do not reflect; do not think about anything at all—I am simply struck of a heap by all this wealth which is lying glittering before my eyes—and I gather up the money mechanically.

I stand outside the counter, stupid with amazement, dumb, paralyzed. I take a stride towards the door, and stop again. I turn my eyes upon a certain spot in the wall, where a little bell is suspended to a leather collar, and underneath this a bundle of string, and I stand and stare at these things.

The shop-boy is struck by the idea that I want to have a chat as I take my time so leisurely, and says, as he tidies a lot of wrapping-papers strewn over the counter:

"It looks as if we were going to have winter snow!"

"Humph! Yes," I reply; "it looks as if we were going to have winter in earnest now; it looks like it," and a while after, I add: "Ah, well, it is none too soon."

I could hear myself speak, but each word I uttered struck my ear as if it were coming from another person. I spoke absolutely unwittingly, involuntarily, without being conscious of myself.

"Oh, do you think so?" says the boy.

I thrust the hand with the money into my pocket, turned the door-handle, and left. I could hear that I said good-night, and that the shop-boy replied to me.

I had gone a few paces away from the shop when the shop-door was torn open, and the boy called after me. I turned round without any astonishment, without a trace of fear; I only collected the money into my hand, and prepared to give it back.

"Beg pardon, you've forgotten your candle," says the boy.

"Ah, thanks," I answered quietly. "Thanks, thanks"; and I strolled on, down the street, bearing it in my hand.

My first sensible thought referred to the money. I went over to a lamp-post, counted it, weighed it in my hand, and smiled. So, in spite of all, I was helped—extraordinarily, grandly, incredibly helped—helped for a long, long time; and I thrust my hand with the money into my pocket, and walked on.

Outside an eating-house in Grand Street I stopped, and turned over in my mind, calmly and quietly, if I should venture so soon to take a little refreshment. I could hear the rattle of knives and plates inside, and the sound of meat being pounded. The temptation was too strong for me—I entered.

"A helping of beef," I say.

"One beef!" calls the waitress down through the door to the lift.

I sat down by myself at a little table next to the door, and prepared to wait. It was somewhat dark where I was sitting, and I felt tolerably well concealed, and set myself to have a serious think. Every now and then the waitress glanced over at me inquiringly. My first downright dishonesty was accomplished—my first theft. Compared to this, all my earlier escapades were as nothing—my first great fall.... Well and good! There was no help for it. For that matter, it was open to me to settle it with the shopkeeper later on, on a more opportune occasion. It need not go any farther with me. Besides that, I had not taken upon myself to live more honourably than all the other folk; there was no contract that....

"Do you think that beef will soon be here?"

"Yes; immediately"; the waitress opens the trapdoor, and looks down into the kitchen.

But suppose the affair did crop up some day? If the shop-boy were to get suspicious and begin to think over the transaction about the bread, and the florin of which the woman got the change? It was not impossible that he would discover it some day, perhaps the next time I went there. Well, then, Lord!... I shrugged my shoulders unobserved.

"If you please," says the waitress, kindly placing the beef on the table, "wouldn't you rather go to another compartment, it's so dark here?"

"No, thanks; just let me be here," I reply; her kindliness touches me at once. I pay for the beef on the spot, put whatever change remains into her hand, close her fingers over it. She smiles, and I say in fun, with the tears near my ears, "There, you're to have the balance to buy yourself a farm.... Ah, you're very welcome to it."

I commenced to eat, got more and more greedy I as I did so,

swallowed whole pieces without chewing them, enjoyed myself in an animal-like way at every mouthful, and tore at the meat like a cannibal.

The waitress came over to me again.

"Will you have anything to drink?" she asks, bending down a little towards me. I looked at her. She spoke very low, almost shyly, and dropped her eyes. "I mean a glass of ale, or whatever you like best ... from me ... without ... that is, if you will...."

"No; many thanks," I answer. "Not now; I shall come back another time."

She drew back, and sat down at the desk. I could only see her head. What a singular creature!

When finished, I made at once for the door. I felt nausea already. The waitress got up. I was afraid to go near the light—afraid to show myself too plainly to the young girl, who never for a moment suspected the depth of my misery; so I wished her a hasty good-night, bowed to her, and left.

The food commenced to take effect. I suffered much from it, and could not keep it down for any length of time. I had to empty my mouth a little at every dark corner I came to. I struggled to master this nausea which threatened to hollow me out anew, clenched my hands, and tried to fight it down; stamped on the pavement, and gulped down furiously whatever sought to come up. All in vain. I sprang at last into a doorway, doubled up, head foremost, blinded with the water which gushed from my eyes, and vomited once more. I was seized with bitterness, and wept as I went along the street.... I cursed the cruel powers, whoever they might be, that persecuted me so, consigned them to hell's damnation and eternal torments for their petty persecution. There was but little chivalry in fate, really little enough chivalry; one was forced to admit that.

I went over to a man staring into a shop-window, and asked him in great haste what, according to his opinion, should one give a man who had been starving for a long time. It was a matter of life and death, I said; he couldn't even keep beef down.

"I have heard say that milk is a good thing—hot milk," answered the man, astonished. "Who is it, by the way, you are asking for?"

"Thanks, thanks," I say; "that idea of hot milk might not be half a bad notion;" and I go.

I entered the first café I came to going along, and asked for some boiled milk. I got the milk, drank it down, hot as it was, swallowed it greedily, every drop, paid for it, and went out again. I took the road home.

Now something singular happened. Outside my door, leaning against the lamp-post, and right under the glare of it, stands a person of whom I get a glimpse from a long distance—it is the lady dressed in black again. The same black-clad lady of the other evenings. There could be no mistake about it; she had turned up at the same spot for the fourth time. She is standing perfectly motionless. I find this so peculiar that I involuntarily slacken my pace. At this moment my thoughts are in good working order, but I am much excited; my nerves are irritated by my last meal. I pass her by as usual; am almost at the door and on the point of entering. There I stop. All of a sudden an inspiration seizes me. Without rendering myself any account of it, I turn round and go straight up to the lady, look her in the face, and bow.

"Good-evening."

"Good-evening," she answers.

Excuse me, was she looking for anything? I had noticed her before; could I be of assistance to her in any way? begged pardon, by-the-way, so earnestly for inquiring.

Yes; she didn't quite know....

No one lived inside that door besides three or four horses and myself; it was, for that matter, only a stable and a tinker's workshop.... She was certainly on a wrong track if she was seeking any one there.

At this she turns her head away, and says: "I am not seeking for anybody. I am only standing here; it was really only a whim. I" ... she stops.

Indeed, really, she only stood there, just stood there, evening after evening, just for a whim's sake!

That was a little odd. I stood and pondered over it, and it perplexed me more and more. I made up my mind to be daring; I jingled my money in my pocket, and asked her, without further ado, to come and have a glass of wine some place or another ... in consideration that winter had come, ha, ha! ... it needn't take very long ... but perhaps she would scarcely....

Ah, no, thanks; she couldn't well do that. No! she couldn't do that; but would I be so kind as to accompany her a little way? She ... it was rather dark to go home now, and she was rather nervous about going up Carl Johann after it got so late.

We moved on; she walked at my right side. A strange, beautiful feeling empowered me; the certainty of being near a young girl. I looked at her the whole way along. The scent of her hair; the warmth that irradiated from her body; the perfume of woman that accompanied her; the sweet breath every time she turned her face towards me—everything penetrated in an ungovernable way through all my senses. So far, I just caught a glimpse of a full, rather pale, face behind the veil, and a high bosom that curved out against her cape. The thought of all the hidden beauty which I surmised lay sheltered under the cloak and veil bewildered me, making me idiotically happy without any reasonable grounds. I could not endure it any longer; I touched her with my hand, passed my fingers over her shoulder, and smiled imbecilely.

"How queer you are," said I.

"Am I, really; in what way?"

Well, in the first place, simply, she had a habit of standing outside a stable door, evening after evening, without any object whatever, just for a whim's sake....

Oh, well, she might have her reason for doing so; besides, she liked staying up late at night; it was a thing she had always had a great fancy for. Did I care about going to bed before twelve?

I? If there was anything in the world I hated it was to go to bed before twelve o'clock at night.

Ah, there, you see! She, too, was just the same; she took this little tour in the evenings when she had nothing to lose by doing so. She lived up in St. Olav's Place.

"Ylajali," I cried.

"I beg pardon?"

"I only said 'Ylajali' ... it's all right. Continue...."

She lived up in St. Olav's Place, lonely enough, together with her mother, to whom one couldn't talk because she was so deaf. Was there anything odd in her liking to get out for a little?

"No, not at all," I replied.

"No? well, what then?"

I could hear by her voice that she was smiling.

Hadn't she a sister?

Yes; an older sister. But, by-the-way, how did I know that? She had gone to Hamburg.

"Lately?"

"Yes; five weeks ago." From where did I learn that she had a sister?

I didn't learn it at all; I only asked.

We kept silence. A man passes us, with a pair of shoes under his arm; otherwise, the street is empty as far as we can see. Over at the Tivoli a long row of coloured lamps are burning. It no longer snows; the sky is clear.

"Gracious! don't you freeze without an overcoat?" inquires the lady, suddenly looking at me.

Should I tell her why I had no overcoat; make my sorry condition known at once, and frighten her away? As well first as last. Still, it was delightful to walk here at her side and keep her in ignorance yet a while longer. So I lied. I answered:

"No, not at all"; and, in order to change the subject, I asked, "Have you seen the menagerie in the Tivoli?"

"No," she answered; "is there really anything to see?"

Suppose she were to take it into her head to wish to go there? Into that blaze of light, with the crowd of people. Why, she would be filled with shame; I would drive her out again, with my shabby clothes, and lean face; perhaps she might even notice that I had no waistcoat on....

"Ah, no; there is sure to be nothing worth seeing!"

And a lot of happy ideas occurred to me, of which I at once made use; a few sparse words, fragments left in my desiccated brain. What would one expect from such a small menagerie? On the whole, it did not interest me in the least to see animals in cases. These animals know that one is standing staring at them; they feel hundreds of inquisitive looks upon them; are conscious of them. No; I would prefer to see animals that didn't know one observed them; shy creatures that nestle in their lair, and lie with sluggish green eyes, and lick their claws, and muse, eh?

Yes; I was certainly right in that.

It was only animals in all their peculiar fearfulness and peculiar savagery that possessed a charm. The soundless, stealthy tread in the total darkness of night; the hidden monsters of the woods; the shrieks of a bird flying past; the wind, the smell of blood, the rumbling in space; in short, the reigning spirit of the kingdom of savage creatures hovering over savagery ... the unconscious poetry!... But I was afraid this bored her. The consciousness of my great poverty seized me anew, and crushed me. If I had only been in any way well-enough dressed to have given her the pleasure of this little tour in the Tivoli! I could not make out this creature, who could find pleasure in letting herself be accompanied up the whole of Carl Johann Street by a half-naked beggar. What, in the name of God, was she thinking of? And why was I walking there, giving myself airs, and smiling idiotically at nothing? Had I any reasonable cause, either, for letting myself be worried into a long walk by this dainty, silken-clad bird? Mayhap it did not cost me an effort? Did I not feel the ice of death go right into my heart at even the gentlest puff of wind that blew against us? Was not madness running riot in my brain, just for lack of food for many months at a stretch? Yet she hindered me from going home to get even a little milk into my parched mouth; a spoonful of sweet milk, that I might perhaps be able to keep down. Why didn't she turn her back on me, and let me go to the deuce?...

I became distracted; my despair reduced me to the last extremity. I said:

"Considering all things, you ought not to walk with me. I disgrace you right under every one's eyes, if only with my clothes. Yes, it is positively true; I mean it."

She starts, looks up quickly at me, and is silent; then she exclaims suddenly:

"Indeed, though!" More she doesn't say.

"What do you mean by that?" I queried.

"Ugh, no; you make me feel ashamed.... We have not got very far now"; and she walked on a little faster.

We turned up University Street, and could already see the lights in

St. Olav's Place. Then she commenced to walk slowly again.

"I have no wish to be indiscreet," I say; "but won't you tell me your name before we part? and won't you, just for one second, lift up your veil so that I can see you? I would be really so grateful."

A pause. I walked on in expectation.

"You have seen me before," she replies.

"Ylajali," I say again.

"Beg pardon. You followed me once for half-a-day, almost right home. Were you tipsy that time?"

I could hear again that she smiled.

"Yes," I said. "Yes, worse luck, I was tipsy that time."

"That was horrid of you!"

And I admitted contritely that it was horrid of me.

We reached the fountains; we stop and look up at the many lighted windows of No. 2.

"Now, you mustn't come any farther with me," she says. "Thank you for coming so far."

I bowed; I daren't say anything; I took off my hat and stood bareheaded. I wonder if she will give me her hand.

"Why don't you ask me to go back a little way with you?" she asks, in a low voice, looking down at the toe of her shoe.

"Great Heavens!" I reply, beside myself, "Great Heavens, if you only would!"

"Yes; but only a little way."

And we turned round.

I was fearfully confused. I absolutely did not know if I were on my head or my heels. This creature upset all my chain of reasoning; turned it topsy-turvy. I was bewitched and extraordinarily happy. It seemed to me as if I were being dragged enchantingly to destruction. She had expressly willed to go back; it wasn't my notion, it was her own desire. I walk on and look at her, and get more and more bold. She encourages me, draws me to her by each word she speaks. I forget for a moment my poverty, my humble position, my whole miserable condition. I feel my blood course madly through my whole body, as in the days before I caved in, and resolved to feel my way by a little ruse.

"By-the-way, it wasn't you I followed that time," said I. "It was your sister."

"Was it my sister?" she questions, in the highest degree amazed. She stands still, looks up at me, and positively waits for an answer. She puts the question in all sober earnest.

"Yes," I replied. "Hum—m, that is to say, it was the younger of the two ladies who went on in front of me."

"The youngest, eh? eh? a-a-ha!" she laughed out all at once, loudly, heartily, like a child. "Oh, how sly you are; you only said that just to get me to raise my veil, didn't you? Ah, I thought so; but you may just wait till you are blue first ... just for punishment."

We began to laugh and jest; we talked incessantly all the time. I do not know what I said, I was so happy. She told me that she had seen me once before, a long time ago, in the theatre. I had then comrades with me, and I behaved like a madman; I must certainly have been tipsy that time too, more's the shame.

Why did she think that?

Oh, I had laughed so.

"Really, a-ah yes; I used to laugh a lot in those days."

"But now not any more?"

"Oh yes; now too. It is a splendid thing to exist sometimes."

We reached Carl Johann. She said: "Now we won't go any farther," and we returned through University Street. When we arrived at the fountain once more I slackened my pace a little; I knew that I could not go any farther with her.

"Well, now you must turn back here," she said, and stopped.

"Yes, I suppose I must."

But a second after she thought I might as well go as far as the door with her. Gracious me, there couldn't be anything wrong in that, could there?

"No," I replied.

But when we were standing at the door all my misery confronted me clearly. How was one to keep up one's courage when one was so broken down? Here I stood before a young lady, dirty, ragged, torn, disfigured by hunger, unwashed, and only half-clad; it was enough to make one sink into the earth. I shrank into myself, bent my head involuntarily, and said:

"May I not meet you any more then?"

I had no hope of being permitted to see her again. I almost wished for a sharp No, that would pull me together a bit and render me callous.

"Yes," she whispered softly, almost inaudibly.

"When?"

"I don't know."

A pause....

"Won't you be so kind as to lift your veil, only just for a minute," I asked. "So that I can see whom I have been talking to. Just for one moment, for indeed I must see whom I have been talking to."

Another pause....

"You can meet me outside here on Tuesday evening," she said. "Will you?"

"Yes, dear lady, if I have permission to."

"At eight o'clock."

"Very well."

I stroked down her cloak with my hand, merely to have an excuse for touching her. It was a delight to me to be so near her.

"And you mustn't think all too badly of me," she added; she was smiling again.

"No."

Suddenly she made a resolute movement and drew her veil up over her forehead; we stood and gazed at one another for a second.

"Ylajali!" I cried. She stretched herself up, flung her arms round my neck and kissed me right on the mouth—only once, swiftly, bewilderingly swiftly, right on the mouth. I could feel how her bosom heaved; she was breathing violently. She wrenched herself suddenly out of my clasp, called a good-night, breathlessly, whispering, and turned and ran up the stairs without a word more....

The hall door shut.

It snowed still more the next day, a heavy snow mingled with rain; great wet flakes that fell to earth and were turned to mud. The air was raw and icy. I woke somewhat late, with my head in a strange state of confusion, my heart intoxicated from the foregone evening by the agitation of that delightful meeting. In my rapture (I had lain a while awake and fancied Ylajali at my side) I spread out my arms and embraced myself and kissed the air. At length I dragged myself out of bed and procured a fresh cup of milk, and straight on top of that a plate of beef. I was no longer hungry, but my nerves were in a highly-strung condition.

I went off to the clothes-shop in the bazaar. It occurred to me that I might pick up a second-hand waistcoat cheaply, something to put on under my coat; it didn't matter what.

I went up the steps to the bazaar and took hold of one and began to examine it.

While I was thus engaged an acquaintance came by; he nodded and called up to me. I let the waistcoat hang and went down to him. He was a designer, and was on the way to his office.

"Come with me and have a glass of beer," he said. "But hurry up, I haven't much time.... What lady was that you were walking with yesterday evening?"

"Listen here now," said I, jealous of his bare thought. "Supposing it was my fiancée."

"By Jove!" he exclaimed.

"Yes; it was all settled yesterday evening."

This nonplussed him completely. He believed me implicitly. I lied in the most accomplished manner to get rid of him. We ordered the beer, drank it, and left.

"Well, good-bye! O listen," he said suddenly. "I owe you a few shillings. It is a shame, too, that I haven't paid you long ago, but now you shall have them during the next few days."

"Yes, thanks," I replied; but I knew that he would never pay me back the few shillings. The beer, I am sorry to say, went almost immediately to my head. The thought of the previous evening's adventure overwhelmed me—made me delirious. Supposing she were not to meet me on Tuesday! Supposing she were to begin to think things over, to get suspicious ... get suspicious of what?... My thoughts gave a jerk and dwelt upon the money. I grew afraid; deadly afraid of myself. The theft rushed in upon me in all its details. I saw the little shop, the counter, my lean hands as I seized the money, and I pictured to myself the line of action the police would adopt when they would come to arrest me. Irons on my hands and feet; no, only on my hands; perhaps only on one hand. The dock, the clerk taking down the evidence, the scratch of his pen—perhaps he might take a new one for the occasion—his look, his threatening look. There, Herr Tangen, to the cell, the eternally dark....

Humph! I clenched my hands tightly to try and summon courage, walked faster and faster, and came to the market-place. There I sat down.

Now, no child's play. How in the wide world could any one prove that I had stolen? Besides, the huckster's boy dare not give an alarm, even if it should occur to him some day how it had all happened. He valued his situation far too dearly for that. No noise, no scenes, may I beg!

But all the same, this money weighed in my pocket sinfully, and gave me no peace. I began to question myself, and I became clearly convinced that I had been happier before, during the period in which I had suffered in all honour. And Ylajali? Had I, too, not polluted her with the touch of my sinful hands? Lord, O Lord my God, Ylajali! I felt as drunk as a bat, jumped up suddenly, and went straight over to the cake woman who was sitting near the chemist's under the sign of the elephant. I might even yet lift myself above dishonour; it was far from being too late; I would show the whole world that I was capable of doing so.

On the way over I got the money in readiness, held every farthing of it in my hand, bent down over the old woman's table as if I wanted something, clapped the money without further ado into her hands. I spoke not a word, turned on my heel, and went my way.

What a wonderful savour there was in feeling oneself an honest man once more! My empty pockets troubled me no longer; it was simply a delightful feeling to me to be cleaned out. When I weighed the whole matter thoroughly, this money had in reality cost me much secret anguish; I had really thought about it with dread and shuddering time upon time. I was no hardened soul; my honourable nature rebelled against such a low action. God be praised, I had raised myself in my own estimation again! "Do as I have done!" I said to myself, looking across the thronged market-place— "only just do as I have done!" I had gladdened a poor old cake vendor to such good purpose that she was perfectly dumbfounded. Tonight her children wouldn't go hungry to bed.... I buoyed myself up with these reflections and considered that I had behaved in a most exemplary manner. God be praised! The money was out of my hands now!

Tipsy and nervous, I wandered down the street, and swelled with satisfaction. The joy of being able to meet Ylajali cleanly and honourably, and of feeling I could look her in the face, ran away with me. I was not conscious of any pain. My head was clear and buoyant; it was as if it were a head of mere light that rested and gleamed on my shoulders. I felt inclined to play the wildest pranks, to do something astounding, to set the whole town in a ferment. All up through Graendsen I conducted myself like a madman. There was a buzzing in my ears, and intoxication ran riot in my brains. The whim seized me to go and tell my age to a commissionaire, who, by-the-way, had not addressed a word to me; to take hold of his hands, and gaze impressively in his face, and leave him again without any explanation. I distinguished every nuance in the voice and laughter of the passers-by, observed some little birds that hopped before me in the street, took to studying the expression of the paving-stones, and discovered all sorts of tokens and signs in them. Thus occupied, I arrive at length at Parliament Place. I stand all at once stock-still, and look at the drosches; the drivers are wandering about, chatting and laughing. The horses hang their heads and cower in the bitter weather. "Go ahead!" I say, giving myself a dig with my elbow. I went hurriedly over to the first vehicle, and got in. "Ullevoldsveien, No. 37," I called out, and we rolled off.

On the way the driver looked round, stooped and peeped several times into the trap, where I sat, sheltered underneath the hood. Had he, too, grown suspicious? There was no doubt of it; my miserable attire had attracted his attention.

"I want to meet a man," I called to him, in order to be beforehand with him, and I explained gravely that I must really meet this man. We stop outside 37, and I jump out, spring up the stairs right to the third storey, seize a bell, and pull it. It gives six or seven fearful peals inside.

A maid comes out and opens the door. I notice that she has round, gold drops in her ears, and black stuff buttons on her grey bodice. She looks at me with a frightened air.

I inquire for Kierulf—Joachim Kierulf, if I might add further—a wool-dealer; in short, not a man one could make a mistake about....

The girl shook her head. "No Kierulf lives here," said she.

She stared at me, and held the door ready to close it. She made no effort to find the man for me. She really looked as if she knew the person I inquired for, if she would only take the trouble to reflect a bit. The lazy jade! I got vexed, turned my back on her, and ran downstairs again.

"He wasn't there," I called to the driver.

"Wasn't he there?"

"No. Drive to Tomtegaden, No. 11." I was in a state of the most violent excitement, and imparted something of the same feeling to the driver. He evidently thought it was a matter of life and death, and he drove on, without further ado. He whipped up the horse sharply.

"What's the man's name?" he inquired, turning round on the box.

"Kierulf, a dealer in wool—Kierulf."

And the driver, too, thought this was a man one would not be likely to make any mistake about.

"Didn't he generally wear a light morning, coat?"

"What!" I cried; "a light morning-coat? Are you mad? Do you think it is a tea-cup I am inquiring about?" This light morning-coat came most inopportunely; it spoilt the whole man for me such as I had fancied him.

"What was it you said he was called?—Kierulf?"

"Of course," I replied. "Is there anything wonderful in that? The name doesn't disgrace any one."

"Hasn't he red hair?"

Well, it was quite possible that he had red hair, and now that the driver mentioned the matter, I was suddenly convinced that he was right. I felt grateful to the poor driver, and hastened to inform him that he had hit the man off to a T—he really was just as he described him,—and I remarked, in addition, that it would be a phenomenon to see such a man without red hair.

"It must be him I drove a couple of times," said the driver; "he had a knobbed stick."

This brought the man vividly before me, and I said, "Ha, ha! I suppose no one has ever yet seen the man without a knobbed stick in his hand, of that you can be certain, quite certain."

Yes, it was clear that it was the same man he had driven. He recognized him—and he drove so that the horse's shoes struck sparks as they touched the stones.

All through this phase of excitement I had not for one second lost my presence of mind. We pass a policeman, and I notice his number is 69. This number struck me with such vivid clearness that it penetrated like a splint into my brain—69—accurately 69. I wouldn't forget it.

I leant back in the vehicle, a prey to the wildest fancies; crouched under the hood so that no one could see me. I moved my lips and commenced to I talk idiotically to myself. Madness rages through my brain, and I let it rage. I am fully conscious that I am succumbing to influences over which I have no control. I begin to laugh, silently, passionately, without a trace of cause, still merry and intoxicated from the couple of glasses of ale I have drunk. Little by little my excitement abates, my calm returns more and more to me. I feel the cold in my sore finger, and I stick it down inside my collar to warm it a little. At length we reach Tomtegaden. The driver pulls up.

I alight, without any haste, absently, listlessly, with my head heavy. I go through a gateway and come into a yard across which I pass. I come to a door which I open and pass through; I find myself in a lobby, a sort of anteroom, with two windows. There are two boxes in it, one on top of the other, in one corner, and against the wall an old, painted sofa-bed over which a rug is spread. To the right, in the next room, I hear voices and the cry of a child, and above me, on the second floor, the sound of an iron plate being hammered. All this I notice the moment as I enter.

I step quietly across the room to the opposite door without any haste, without any thought of flight; open it, too, and come out in Vognmansgaden. I look up at the house through which I have passed. "Refreshment and lodgings for travellers."

It is not my intention to escape, to steal away from the driver who is waiting for me. I go very coolly down Vognmansgaden, without fear of being conscious of doing any wrong. Kierulf, this dealer in wool, who has spooked in my brain so long—this creature in whose existence I believe, and whom it was of vital importance that I should meet—had vanished from my memory; was wiped out with many other mad whims which came and went in turns. I recalled him no longer, except as a reminiscence—a phantom.

In measure, as I walked on, I become more and more sober; felt languid and weary, and dragged my legs after me. The snow still fell in great moist flakes. At last I reached Gronland; far out, near the church, I sat down to rest on a seat. All the passers-by looked at me with much astonishment. I fell a-thinking.

Thou good God, what a miserable plight I have come to! I was so heartily tired and weary of all my miserable life that I did not find it worth the trouble of fighting any longer to preserve it. Adversity had gained the upper hand; it had been too strong for me. I had become so strangely poverty-stricken and broken, a mere shadow of what I once had been; my shoulders were sunken right down on one side, and I had contracted a habit of stooping forward fearfully as I walked, in order to spare my chest what little I could. I had examined my body a few days ago, one noon up in my room, and I had stood and cried over it the whole time. I had worn the same shirt for many weeks, and it was quite stiff with stale sweat, and had chafed my skin. A little blood and water ran out of the sore place; it did not hurt much, but it was very tiresome to have this tender place in the middle of my stomach. I had no remedy for it, and it wouldn't heal of its own accord. I washed it, dried it carefully, and put on the same shirt. There was no help for it, it....

I sit there on the bench and ponder over all this, and am sad enough. I loathe myself. My very hands seem distasteful to me; the loose, almost coarse, expression of the backs of them pains me, disgusts me. I feel myself rudely affected by the sight of my lean fingers. I hate the whole of my gaunt, shrunken body, and shrink from bearing it, from feeling it envelop me. Lord, if the whole thing would come to an end now, I would heartily, gladly die!

Completely worsted, soiled, defiled, and debased in my own estimation, I rose mechanically and commenced to turn my steps homewards. On the way I passed a door, upon which the following was to be read on a plate— "Winding-sheets to be had at Miss Andersen's, door to the right." Old memories! I muttered, as my thoughts flew back to my former room in Hammersborg. The little rocking-chair, the newspapers near the door, the lighthouse director's announcement, and Fabian Olsen, the baker's new-baked bread. Ah yes; times were better with me then than now; one night I had written a tale for ten shillings, now I couldn't write anything. My head grew light as soon as ever I attempted it. Yes, I would put an end to it now; and I went on and on.

As I got nearer and nearer to the provision shop, I had the half-conscious feeling of approaching a danger, but I determined to stick to my purpose; I would give myself up. I ran quickly up the steps. At the door I met a little girl who was carrying a cup in her hands, and I slipped past her and opened the door. The shop boy and I stand face to face alone for the second time.

"Well!" he exclaims; "fearfully bad weather now, isn't it?" What did this going round the bush signify? Why didn't he seize me at once? I got furious, and cried:

"Oh, I haven't come to prate about the weather."

This violent preliminary takes him aback; his little huckster brain fails him. It has never even occurred to him that I have cheated him of five shillings.

"Don't you know, then, that I have swindled you?" I query impatiently, and I breathe quickly with the excitement; I tremble and am ready to use force if he doesn't come to the point.

But the poor man has no misgivings.

Well, bless my soul, what stupid creatures one has to mix with in this world! I abuse him, explain to him every detail as to how it had all happened, show him where the fact was accomplished, where the money had lain; how I had gathered it up in my hand and closed my fingers over it— and he takes it all in and does nothing. He shifts uneasily from one foot to the other, listens for footsteps in the next room, make signs to hush me, to try and make me speak lower, and says at last:

"It was a mean enough thing of you to do!"

"No; hold on," I explained in my desire to contradict him—to aggravate him. It wasn't quite so mean as he imagined it to be, in his huckster head. Naturally, I didn't keep the money; that could never have entered my head. I, for my part, scorned to derive any benefit from it—that was opposed to my thoroughly honest nature.

"What did you do with it, then?"

"I gave it away to a poor old woman—every farthing of it." He must understand that that was the sort of person I was; I didn't forget the poor so....

He stands and thinks over this a while, becomes manifestly very dubious as to how far I am an honest man or not. At last he says:

"Oughtn't you rather to have brought it back again?"

"Now, listen here," I reply; "I didn't want to get you into trouble in any way; but that is the thanks one gets for being generous. Here I stand and explain the whole thing to you, and you simply, instead of being ashamed as a dog, make no effort to settle the dispute with me. Therefore I wash my hands of you, and as for the rest, I say, 'The devil take you!' Good-day."

I left, slamming the door behind me. But when I got home to my room, into the melancholy hole, wet through from the soft snow, trembling in my knees from the day's wanderings, I dismounted instantly from my high horse, and sank together once more.

I regretted my attack upon the poor shop-boy, wept, clutched myself by the throat to punish myself for my miserable trick, and behaved like a lunatic. He had naturally been in the most deadly terror for the sake of his situation; he had not dared to make any fuss about the five shillings that were lost to the business, and I had taken advantage of his fear, had tortured him with my violent address, stabbed him with every loud word that I had roared out. And the master himself had perhaps been sitting inside the inner room, almost within an ace of feeling called upon to come out and inquire what was the row. No, there was no longer any limit to the low things I might be tempted to do.

Well, why hadn't I been locked up? then it would have come to an end. I would almost have stretched out my wrists for the handcuffs. I would not have offered the slightest resistance; on the contrary, I would have assisted them. Lord of Heaven and Earth! one day of my life for one happy second again! My whole life for a mess of lentils! Hear me only this once!...

I laid down in the wet clothes I had on, with a vague idea that I might die during the night. And I used my last strength to tidy up my bed a little, so that it might appear a little orderly about me in the morning. I folded my hands and chose my position.

All at once I remember Ylajali. To think that I could have forgotten her the entire evening through! And light forces its way ever so faintly into my spirit again—a little ray of sunshine that makes me so blessedly warm; and gradually more sun comes, a rare, silken, balmy light that caresses me with soothing loveliness. And the sun grows stronger and stronger, burns sharply in my temples, seethes fiercely and glowingly in my emaciated brain. And at last, a maddening pyre of rays flames up before my eyes; a heaven and earth in conflagration men and beasts of fire, mountains of fire, devils of fire, an abyss, a wilderness, a hurricane, a universe in brazen ignition, a smoking, smouldering day of doom!

And I saw and heard no more....

I woke in a sweat the next morning, moist all over, my whole body bathed in dampness. The fever had laid violent hands on me. At first I had no clear idea of what had happened to me; I looked about me in amazement, felt a complete transformation of my being, absolutely failed to recognize myself again. I felt along my own arms and down my legs, was struck with astonishment that the window was where it was, and not in the opposite wall; and I could hear the tramp of the horses' feet in the yard below as if it came from above me. I felt rather sick, too—qualmish.

My hair clung wet and cold about my forehead. I raised myself on my elbow and looked at the pillow; damp hair lay on it, too, in patches. My feet had swelled up in my shoes during the night, but they caused me no pain, only I could not move my toes much, they were too stiff.

As the afternoon closed in, and it had already begun to grow a little dusk, I got up out of bed and commenced to move about the room a little. I felt my way with short, careful steps, taking care to keep my balance and spare my feet as much as possible. I did not suffer much, and I did not cry; neither was I, taking all into consideration, sad. On the contrary, I was blissfully content. It did not strike me just then that anything could be otherwise than it was.

Then I went out.

The only thing that troubled me a little, in spite of the nausea that the thought of food inspired in me, was hunger. I commenced to be sensible of a shameless appetite again; a ravenous lust of food, which grew steadily worse and worse. It gnawed unmercifully in my breast; carrying on a silent, mysterious work in there. It was as if a score of diminutive gnome-like insects set their heads on one side and gnawed for a little, then laid their heads on the other side and gnawed a little more, then lay quite still for a moment's space, and then began afresh, boring noiselessly in, and without any haste, and left empty spaces everywhere after them as they went on....

I was not ill, but faint; I broke into a sweat. I thought of going to the market-place to rest a while, but the way was long and wearisome; at last I had almost reached it. I stood at the corner of the market and Market Street; the sweat ran down into my eyes and blinded me, and I had just stopped in order to wipe it away a little. I did not notice the place I was standing in; in fact, I did not think about it; the noise around me was something frightful.

Suddenly a call rings out, a cold, sharp warning. I hear this cry—hear it quite well, and I start nervously to one side, stepping as quickly as my bad foot allows me to. A monster of a bread-van brushes past me, and the wheel grazes my coat; I might perhaps have been a little quicker if I had exerted myself. Well, there was no help for it; one foot pained me, a couple of toes were crunched. I felt that they, as it were, curled up in my shoes.

The driver reins in his horse with all his might. He turns round on the van and inquires in a fright how it fares with me. Oh! it might have been worse, far worse.... It was perhaps not so dangerous.... I didn't think any bones were broken. Oh, pray....

I rushed over as quickly as I could to a seat; all these people who stopped and stared at me abashed me. After all, it was no mortal blow; comparatively speaking, I had got off luckily enough, as misfortune was bound to come in my way. The worst thing was that my shoe was crushed to pieces; the sole was torn loose at the toe. I help up my foot, and saw blood inside the gap. Well, it wasn't intentional on either side; it was not the man's purpose to make things worse for me than they were; he looked much concerned about it. It was quite certain that if I had begged him for a piece of bread out of his cart he would have given it to me. He would certainly have given it to me gladly. God bless him in return, wherever he is!...

I was terribly hungry, and I did not know what to do with myself and my shameless appetite. I writhed from side to side on the seat, and bowed my chest right down to my knees; I was almost distracted. When it got dark I jogged along to the Town Hall—God knows how I got there—and sat on the edge of the balustrade. I tore a pocket out of my coat and took to chewing it; not with any defined object, but with dour mien and unseeing eyes, staring straight into space. I could hear a group of little children playing around near me, and perceive, in an instinctive sort of way, some pedestrians pass me by; otherwise I observed nothing.

All at once, it enters my head to go to one of the meat bazaars underneath me, and beg a piece of raw meat. I go straight along the balustrade to the other side of the bazaar buildings, and descend the steps. When I had nearly reached the stalls on the lower floor, I called up the archway leading to the stairs, and made a threatening backward gesture, as if I were talking to a dog up there, and boldly addressed the first butcher I met.

"Ah, will you be kind enough to give me a bone for my dog?" I said; "only a bone. There needn't be anything on it; it's just to give him something to carry in his mouth."

I got the bone, a capital little bone, on which there still remained a morsel of meat, and hid it under my coat. I thanked the man so heartily that he looked at me in amazement.

"Oh, no need of thanks," said he.

"Oh yes; don't say that," I mumbled; "it is kindly done of you," and I ascended the steps again.

My heart was throbbing violently in my breast. I sneaked into one of the passages, where the forges are, as far in as I could go, and stopped outside a dilapidated door leading to a back-yard. There was no light to be seen anywhere, only blessed darkness all around me; and I began to gnaw at the bone.

It had no taste; a rank smell of blood oozed from it, and I was forced to vomit almost immediately. I tried anew. If I could only keep it down, it would, in spite of all, have some effect. It was simply a matter of forcing it to remain down there. But I vomited again. I grew wild, bit angrily into the meat, tore off a morsel, and gulped it down by sheer strength of will; and yet it was of no use. Just as soon as the little fragments of meat became warm in my stomach up they came again, worse luck. I clenched my hands in frenzy, burst into tears from sheer helplessness, and gnawed away as one possessed. I cried, so that the bone got wet and dirty with my tears, vomited, cursed and groaned again, cried as if my heart would break, and vomited anew. I consigned all the powers that be to the lowermost torture in the loudest voice.

Quiet—not a soul about—no light, no noise; I am in a state of the most fearful excitement; I breathe hardly and audibly, and I cry with gnashing teeth, each time that the morsel of meat, which might satisfy me a little, comes up. As I find that, in spite of all my efforts, it avails me naught, I cast the bone at the door. I am filled with the most impotent hate; shriek, and menace with my fists towards Heaven; yell God's name hoarsely, and bend my fingers like claws, with ill-suppressed fury....

I tell you, you Heaven's Holy Baal, you don't exist; but that, if you did, I would curse you so that your Heaven would quiver with the fire of hell! I tell you, I have offered you my service, and you repulsed me; and I turn my back on you for all eternity, because you did not know your time of visitation! I tell you that I am about to die, and yet I mock you! You Heaven God and Apis! with death staring me in the face—I tell you, I would rather be a bondsman in hell than a freedman in your mansions! I tell you, I am filled with a blissful contempt for your divine paltriness; and I choose the abyss of destruction for a perpetual resort, where the devils Judas and Pharaoh are cast down!

I tell you your Heaven is full of the kingdom of the earth's most crass-headed idiots and poverty-stricken in spirit! I tell you, you have filled your Heaven with the grossest and most cherished harlots from here below, who have bent their knees piteously before you at their hour of death! I tell you, you have used force against me, and you know not, you omniscient nullity, that I never bend in opposition! I tell you, all my life, every cell in my body, every power of my soul, gasps to mock you—you Gracious Monster on High. I tell you, I would, if I could, breathe it into every human soul, every flower, every leaf, every dewdrop in the garden! I tell you, I would scoff you on the day of doom, and curse the teeth out of my mouth for the sake of your Deity's boundless miserableness! I tell you from this hour I renounce all thy works and all thy pomps! I will execrate my thought if it dwell on you again, and tear out my lips if they ever utter your name! I tell you, if you exist, my last word in life or in death—I bid you farewell, for all time and eternity—I bid you farewell with heart and reins. I bid you the last irrevocable farewell, and I am silent, and turn my back on you and go my way.... Quiet.

I tremble with excitement and exhaustion, and stand on the same spot, still whispering oaths and abusive epithets, hiccoughing after the violent crying fit, broken down and apathetic after my frenzied outburst of rage. I stand there for maybe an hour, hiccough and whisper, and hold on to the door. Then I hear voices—a conversation between two men who are coming down the passage. I slink away from the door, drag myself along the walls of the houses, and come out again into the light streets. As I jog along Young's Hill my brain begins to work in a most peculiar direction. It occurs to me that the wretched hovels down at the corner of the market-place, the stores for loose materials, the old booths for second-hand clothes, are really a disgrace to the place—they spoilt the whole appearance of the market, and were a blot on the town, Fie! away with the rubbish! And I turned over in my mind as I walked on what it would cost to remove the Geographical Survey down there—that handsome building which had always attracted me so much each time I passed it. It would perhaps not be possible to undertake a removal of that kind under two or three hundred pounds. A pretty sum—three hundred pounds! One must admit, a tidy enough little sum for pocket-money! Ha, ha! just to make a start with, eh? and I nodded my head, and conceded that it was a tidy enough bit of pocket-money to make a start with. I was still trembling over my whole body, and hiccoughed now and then violently after my cry. I had a feeling that there was not much life left in me—that I was really singing my last verse. It was almost a matter of indifference to me; it did not trouble me in the least. On the contrary, I wended my way down town, down to the wharf, farther and farther away from my room. I would, for that matter, have willingly laid myself down flat in the street to die. My sufferings were rendering me more and more callous. My sore foot throbbed violently; I had a sensation as if the pain was creeping up through my whole leg. But not even that caused me any particular distress. I had endured worse sensations.

In this manner, I reached the railway wharf. There was no traffic, no noise—only here and there a person to be seen, a labourer or sailor slinking round with their hands in their pockets. I took notice of a lame man, who looked sharply at me as we passed one another. I stopped him instinctively, touched my hat, and inquired if he knew if the Nun had sailed. Someway, I couldn't help snapping my fingers right under the man's nose, and saying, "Ay, by Jove, the Nun; yes, the Nun!" which I had totally forgotten. All the same, the thought of her had been smouldering in me. I had carried it about unconsciously.

Yes, bless me, the Nun had sailed.

He couldn't tell me where she had sailed to?

The man reflects, stands on his long leg, keeps the other up in the air; it dangles a little.

"No," he replies. "Do you know what cargo she was taking in here?"

"No," I answer. But by this time I had already lost interest in the Nun, and I asked the man how far it might be to Holmestrand, reckoned in good old geographical miles.

"To Holmestrand? I should think..."

"Or to Vœblungsnaess?"

"What was I going to say? I should think to Holmestrand..."

"Oh, never mind; I have just remembered it," I interrupted him again. "You wouldn't perhaps be so kind as to give me a small bit of tobacco—only just a tiny scrap?"

I received the tobacco, thanked the man heartily, and went on. I made no use of the tobacco; I put it into my pocket. He still kept his eye on me— perhaps I had aroused his suspicions in some other way or another. Whether I stood still or walked on, I felt his suspicious look following me. I had no mind to be persecuted by this creature. I turn round, and, dragging myself back to him, say:

"Binder"—only this one word, "Binder!" no more. I looked fixedly at him as I say it, indeed I was conscious of staring fearfully at him. It was as if I saw him with my entire body instead of only with my eyes. I stare for a while after I give utterance to this word, and then I jog along again to the railway square. The man does not utter a syllable, he only keeps his gaze fixed upon me.

"Binder!" I stood suddenly still. Yes, wasn't that just what I had a feeling of the moment I met the old chap; a feeling that I had met him before! One bright morning up in Graendsen, when I pawned my waistcoat. It seemed to me an eternity since that day.

Whilst I stand and ponder over this, I lean and support myself against a house wall at the corner of the railway square and Harbour Street. Suddenly, I start quickly and make an effort to crawl away. As I do not succeed in it, I stare case-hardened ahead of me and fling all shame to the winds. There is no help for it. I am standing face to face with the "Commodore." I get devil-may-care—brazen. I take yet a step farther from the wall in order to make him notice me. I do not do it to awake his compassion, but to mortify myself, place myself, as it were, on the pillory. I could have flung myself down in the street and begged him to walk over me, tread on my face. I don't even bid him good-evening.

Perhaps the "Commodore" guesses that something is amiss with me. He slackens his pace a little, and I say, in order to stop him, "I would have called upon you long ago with something, but nothing has come yet!"

"Indeed?" he replies in an interrogative tone. "You haven't got it finished, then?"

"No, it didn't get finished."

My eyes by this time are filled with tears at his friendliness, and I cough with a bitter effort to regain my composure. The "Commodore" tweaks his nose and looks at me.

"Have you anything to live on in the meantime?" he questions.

"No," I reply. "I haven't that either; I haven't eaten anything today, but...."

"The Lord preserve you, man, it will never do for you to go and starve yourself to death," he exclaims, feeling in his pocket.

This causes a feeling of shame to awake in me, and I stagger over to the wall and hold on to it. I see him finger in his purse, and he hands me half-a-sovereign.

He makes no fuss about it, simply gives me half-a-sovereign, reiterating at the same time that it would never do to let me starve to death. I stammered an objection and did not take it all at once. It is shameful of me to ... it was really too much....

"Hurry up," he says, looking at his watch. "I have been waiting for the train; I hear it coming now."

I took the money; I was dumb with joy, and never said a word; I didn't even thank him once.

"It isn't worth while feeling put out about it," said the "Commodore" at last. "I know you can write for it."

And so off he went.

When he had gone a few steps, I remembered all at once that I had not thanked him for this great assistance. I tried to overtake him, but could not get on quickly enough; my legs failed me, and I came near tumbling on my face. He went farther and farther away from me. I gave up the attempt; thought of calling after him, but dared not; and when after all I did muster up courage enough and called once or twice, he was already at too great a distance, and my voice had become too weak.

I was left standing on the pavement, gazing after him. I wept quietly and silently. "I never saw the like!" I said to myself. "He gave me half-a-sovereign." I walked back and placed myself where he had stood, imitated all his movements held the half-sovereign up to my moistened eyes, inspected it on both sides, and began to swear—to swear at the top of my voice, that there was no manner of doubt that what I held in my hand was half-a-sovereign. An hour after, maybe—a very long hour, for it had grown very silent all around me—I stood, singularly enough, outside No. 11 Tomtegaden. After I had stood and collected my wits for a moment and wondered thereat, I went through the door for the second time, right into the "Entertainment and lodgings for travellers." Here I asked for shelter and was immediately supplied with a bed.

Tuesday.

Sunshine and quiet—a strangely bright day. The snow had disappeared. There was life and joy, and glad faces, smiles, and laughter everywhere. The fountains threw up sprays of water in jets, golden-tinted from the sun-light, azure from the sky....

At noon I left my lodgings in Tomtegaden, where I still lived and found fairly comfortable, and set out for town. I was in the merriest humour, and lazied about the whole afternoon through the most frequented streets and looked at the people. Even before seven o'clock I took a turn up St. Olav's Place and took a furtive look up at the window of No. 2. In an hour I would see her. I went about the whole time in a state of tremulous, delicious dread. What would happen? What should I say when she came down the stairs? Good-evening? or only smile? I concluded to let it rest with the smile. Of course I would bow profoundly to her.

I stole away, a little ashamed to be there so early, wandered up Carl Johann for a while, and kept my eyes on University Street. When the clocks struck eight I walked once more towards St. Olav's Place. On the way it struck me that perhaps I might arrive a few minutes too late, and I quickened my pace as much as I could. My foot was very sore, otherwise nothing ailed me.

I took up my place at the fountain and drew breath. I stood there a long while and gazed up at the window of No. 2, but she did not come. Well, I would wait; I was in no hurry. She might be delayed, and I waited on. It couldn't well be that I had dreamt the whole thing! Had my first meeting with her only existed in imagination the night I lay in delirium? I began in perplexity to think over it, and wasn't at all sure.

"Hem!" came from behind me. I heard this, and I also heard light steps near me, but I did not turn round, I only stared up at the wide staircase before me.

"Good-evening," came then. I forget to smile; I don't even take off my hat at first, I am so taken aback to see her come this way.

"Have you been waiting long?" she asks. She is breathing a little quickly after her walk.

"No, not at all; I only came a little while ago," I reply. "And besides, would it matter if I had waited long? I expected, by-the-way, that you would come from another direction."

"I accompanied mamma to some people. Mamma is spending the evening with them."

"Oh, indeed," I say.

We had begun to walk on involuntarily. A policeman is standing at the corner, looking at us.

"But, after all, where are we going to?" she asks, and stops.

"Wherever you wish; only where you wish."

"Ugh, yes! but it's such a bore to have to decide oneself."

A pause.

Then I say, merely for the sake of saying something:

"I see it's dark up in your windows."

"Yes, it is," she replies gaily; "the servant has an evening off, too, so I am all alone at home."

We both stand and look up at the windows of No. 2 as if neither of us had seen them before.

"Can't we go up to your place, then?" I say; "I shall sit down at the door the whole time if you like."

But then I trembled with emotion, and regretted greatly that I had perhaps been too forward. Supposing she were to get angry, and leave me. Suppose I were never to see her again. Ah, that miserable attire of mine! I waited despairingly for her reply.

"You shall certainly not sit down by the door," she says. She says it right down tenderly, and says accurately these words: "You shall certainly not sit down by the door."

We went up.

Out on the lobby, where it was dark, she took hold of my hand, and led me on. There was no necessity for my being so quiet, she said, I could very well talk. We entered. Whilst she lit the candle—it was not a lamp she lit, but a candle—whilst she lit the candle, she said, with a little laugh:

"But now you mustn't look at me. Ugh! I am so ashamed, but I will never do it again."

"What will you never do again?"

"I will never ... ugh ... no ... good gracious ... I will never kiss you again!"

"Won't you?" I said, and we both laughed. I stretched out my arms to her, and she glided away; slipped round to the other side of the table. We stood a while and gazed at one another; the candle stood right between us.

"Try and catch me," she said; and with much laughter I tried to seize hold of her. Whilst she sprang about, she loosened her veil, and took off her hat; her sparkling eyes hung on mine, and watched my movements. I made a fresh sortie, and tripped on the carpet and fell, my sore foot refusing to bear me up any longer. I rose in extreme confusion.

"Lord, how red you did get!" she said. "Well it was awfully awkward of you."

"Yes, it was," I agreed, and we began the chase afresh.

"It seems to me you limp."

"Yes; perhaps I do—just a little—only just a little, for that matter."

"Last time you had a sore finger, now you have got a sore foot; it is awful the number of afflictions you have."

"Ah, yes. I was run over slightly, a few days ago."

"Run over! Tipsy again? Why, good heavens! what a life you lead, young man!" and she threatened me with her forefinger, and tried to appear grave. "Well, let us sit down, then; no, not down there by the door; you are far too reserved! Come here—you there, and I here—so, that's it ... ugh, it's such a bore with reticent people! One has to say and do everything oneself; one gets no help to do anything. Now, for example, you might just as well put your arm over the back of my chair; you could easily have thought of that much out of your own head, couldn't you? But if I say anything like that, you open your eyes as wide as if you couldn't believe what was being said. Yes, it is really true; I have noticed it several times; you are doing it now, too; but you needn't try to persuade me that you are always so modest; it is only when you don't dare to be otherwise than quiet. You were daring enough the day you were tipsy—when you followed me straight home and worried me with your witticisms. 'You are losing your book, madam; you are quite certainly losing your book, madam!' Ha, ha, ha! it was really shameless of you."

I sat dejectedly and looked at her; my heart beat violently, my blood raced quickly through my veins, there was a singular sense of enjoyment in it!

"Why don't you say something?"

"What a darling you are," I cried. "I am simply sitting here getting thoroughly fascinated by you—here this very moment thoroughly fascinated.... There is no help for it.... You are the most extraordinary creature that ... sometimes your eyes gleam so, that I never saw their match; they look like flowers ... eh? No, well, no, perhaps, not like flowers, either, but ... I am so desperately in love with you, and it is so preposterous ... for, great Scott! there is naturally not an atom of a chance for me.... What is your name? Now, you really must tell me what you are called."

"No; what is your name? Gracious, I was nearly forgetting that again! I thought about it all yesterday, that I meant to ask you—yes, that is to say, not all yesterday, but—"

"Do you know what I named you? I named you Ylajali. How do you like that? It has a gliding sound...."

"Ylajali?"

"Yes."

"Is that a foreign language?"

"Humph—no, it isn't that either!"

"Well, it isn't ugly!"

After a long discussion we told one another our names. She seated herself close to my side on the sofa, and shoved the chair away with her foot, and we began to chatter afresh.

"You are shaved this evening, too," she said; look on the whole a little better than the last time—that is to say, only just a scrap better. Don't imagine ... no; the last time you were really shabby, and you had a dirty rag round your finger into the bargain; and in that state you absolutely wanted me to go to some place, and take wine with you—thanks, not me!"

"So it was, after all, because of my miserable appearance that you would not go with me?" I said.

"No," she replied and looked down. "No; God knows it wasn't. I didn't even think about it."

"Listen," said I; "you are evidently sitting here labouring under the delusion that I can dress and live exactly as I choose, aren't you? And that is just what I can't do; I am very, very poor."

She looked at me. "Are you?" she queried.

"Yes, worse luck, I am."

After an interval.

"Well, gracious, so am I, too," she said, with a cheerful movement of her head.

Every one of her words intoxicated me, fell on my heart like drops of wine. She enchanted me with the trick she had of putting her head a little on one side, and listening when I said anything, and I could feel her breath brush my face.

"Do you know," I said, "that ... but, now, you mustn't get angry—when I went to bed last night I settled this arm for you ... so ... as if you lay on it ... and then I went to sleep."

"Did you? That was lovely!" A pause. "But of course it could only be from a distance that you would venture to do such a thing, for otherwise...."

"Don't you believe I could do it otherwise?"

"No, I don't believe it."

"Ah, from me you may expect everything," I said, and I put my arm around her waist.

"Can I?" was all she said.

It annoyed me, almost wounded me, that she should look upon me as being so utterly inoffensive. I braced myself up, steeled my heart, and seized her hand; but she withdrew it softly, and moved a little away from me. That just put an end to my courage again; I felt ashamed, and looked out through the window. I was, in spite of all, in far too wretched a condition; I must, above all, not try to imagine myself any one in particular. It would have been another matter if I had met her during the time that I still looked like a respectable human being—in my old, well-off days when I had sufficient to make an appearance; and I felt fearfully downcast!

"There now, one can see!" she said, "now one can just see one can snub you with just the tiniest frown—make you look sheepish by just moving a little away from you" ... she laughed, tantalizingly, roguishly, with tightly-closed eyes, as if she could not stand being looked at, either.

"Well, upon my soul!" I blurted out, "now you shall just see," and I flung my arms violently around her shoulders. I was mortified. Was the girl out of her senses? Did she think I was totally inexperienced! Ha! Then I would, by the living.... No one should say of me that I was backward on that score. The creature was possessed by the devil himself! If it were only a matter of going at it, well....

She sat quite quietly, and still kept her eyes closed; neither of us spoke. I crushed her fiercely to me, pressed her body greedily against my breast, and she spoke never a word. I heard her heart's beat, both hers and mine; they sounded like hurrying hoof-beats.

I kissed her.

I no longer knew myself. I uttered some nonsense, that she laughed at, whispered pet names into her mouth, caressed her cheek, kissed her many times....

She winds her arms about my neck, quite slowly, tenderly, the breath of her pink quivering nostrils fans me right in the face; she strokes down my shoulders with her left hand, and says, "What a lot of loose hair there is."

"Yes," I reply.

"What can be the reason that your hair falls out so?"

"Don't know."

"Ah, of course, because you drink too much, and perhaps ... fie, I won't say it. You ought to be ashamed. No, I wouldn't have believed that of you! To think that you, who are so young, already should lose your hair! Now, do please just tell me what sort of way you really spend your life—I am certain it is dreadful! But only the truth, do you hear; no evasions. Anyway, I shall see by you if you hide anything—there, tell now!"

"Yes; but let me kiss you first, then."

"Are you mad?... Humph, ... I want to hear what kind of a man you are.... Ah, I am sure it is dreadful."

It hurt me that she should believe the worst of me; I was afraid of thrusting her away entirely, and I could not endure the misgivings she had as to my way of life. I would clear myself in her eyes, make myself worthy of her, show her that she was sitting at the side of a person almost angelically disposed. Why, bless me, I could count my falls up to date on my fingers. I related—related all—and I only related truth. I made out nothing any worse than it was; it was not my intention to rouse her compassion. I told her also that I had stolen five shillings one evening.

She sat and listened, with open mouth, pale, frightened, her shining eyes completely bewildered. I desired to make it good again, to disperse the sad impression I had made, and I pulled myself up.

"Well, it is all over now!" I said; "there can be no talk of such a thing happening again; I am saved now...."

But she was much dispirited. "The Lord preserve me!" was all she said, then kept silent. She repeated this at short intervals, and kept silent after each "the Lord preserve me."

I began to jest, caught hold of her, tried to tickle her, lifted her up to my breast. I was irritated not a little—indeed, downright hurt. Was I more unworthy in her eyes now, than if I had myself been instrumental in causing the falling out of my hair? Would she have thought more of me if I had made myself out to be a roué?... No nonsense now;... it was just a matter of going at it; and if it was only just a matter of going at it, so, by the living...

"No;... what do you want?" she queried, and she added these distressing words, "I can't be sure that you are not insane!"

I checked myself involuntarily, and I said: "You don't mean that!"

"Indeed, God knows I do! you look so strangely. And the forenoon you followed me—after all, you weren't tipsy that time?"

"No; but I wasn't hungry then, either; I had just eaten...."

"Yes; but that made it so much the worse."

"Would you rather I had been tipsy?"

"Yes ... ugh ... I am afraid of you! Lord, can't you let me be now!"

I considered a moment. No, I couldn't let her be.... I happened, as if inadvertently, to knock over the light, so that it went out. She made a despairing struggle—gave vent at last to a little whimper.

"No, not that! If you like, you may rather kiss me, oh, dear, kind...."

I stopped instantly. Her words sounded so terrified, so helpless, I was struck to the heart. She meant to offer me a compensation by giving me leave to kiss her! How charming, how charmingly naïve. I could have fallen down and knelt before her.

"But, dear pretty one," I said, completely bewildered, "I don't understand.... I really can't conceive what sort of a game this is...."

She rose, lit the candle again with trembling hands. I leant back on the sofa and did nothing. What would happen now? I was in reality very ill at ease.

She cast a look over at the clock on the wall, and started.

"Ugh, the girl will soon come now!" she said; this was the first thing she said. I took the hint, and rose. She took up her jacket as if to put it on, bethought herself, and let it lie, and went over to the fireplace. So that it should not appear as if she had shown me the door, I said:

"Was your father in the army?" and at the same time I prepared to leave.

"Yes; he was an officer. How did you know?"

"I didn't know; it just came into my head."

"That was odd."

"Ah, yes; there were some places I came to where I got a kind of presentiment. Ha, ha!—a part of my insanity, eh?"

She looked quickly up, but didn't answer. I felt I worried her with my presence, and determined to make short work of it. I went towards the door. Would she not kiss me any more now? not even give me her hand? I stood and waited.

"Are you going now, then?" she said, and yet she remained quietly standing over near the fireplace.

I did not reply. I stood humbly in confusion, and looked at her without saying anything. Why hadn't she left me in peace, when nothing was to come of it? What was the matter with her now? It didn't seem to put her out that I stood prepared to leave. She was all at once completely lost to me, and I searched for something to say to her in farewell—a weighty, cutting word that would strike her, and perhaps impress her a little. And in the face of my first resolve, hurt as I was, instead of being proud and cold, disturbed and offended, I began right off to talk of trifles. The telling word would not come; I conducted myself in an exceedingly aimless fashion. Why couldn't she just as well tell me plainly and straightly to go my way? I queried. Yes, indeed, why not? There was no need of feeling embarrassed about it. Instead of reminding me that the girl would soon come home, she could have simply said as follows: "Now you must run, for I must go and fetch my mother, and I won't have your escort through the street." So it was not that she had been thinking about? Ah, yes; it was that all the same she had thought about; I understood that at once. It did not require much to put me on the right track; only, just the way she had taken up her jacket, and left it down again, had convinced me immediately. As I said before, I had presentiments; and it was not altogether insanity that was at the root of it....

"But, great heavens! do forgive me for that word! It slipped out of my mouth," she cried; but yet she stood quite quietly, and did not come over to me.

I was inflexible, and went on. I stood there and prattled, with the painful consciousness that I bored her, that not one of my words went home, and all the same I did not cease.

At bottom one might be a fairly sensitive nature, even if one were not insane, I ventured to say. There were natures that fed on trifles, and died just for one hard word's sake; and I implied that I had such a nature. The fact was, that my poverty had in that degree sharpened certain powers in me, so that they caused me unpleasantness. Yes, I assure you honestly, unpleasantness; worse luck! But this had also its advantages. It helped me in certain situations in life. The poor intelligent man is a far nicer observer than the rich intelligent man. The poor man looks about him at every step he takes, listens suspiciously to every word he hears from the people he meets, every step he takes affords in this way a task for his thoughts and feelings—an occupation. He is quick of hearing, and sensitive; he is an experienced man, his soul bears the sears of the fire....

And I talked a long time over these sears my soul had. But the longer I talked, the more troubled she grew. At last she muttered, "My God!" a couple of times in despair, and wrung her hands. I could see well that I tormented her, and I had no wish to torment her—but did it, all the same. At last, being of the opinion that I had succeeded in telling her in rude enough terms the essentials of what I had to say, I was touched by her heart-stricken expression. I cried:

"Now I am going, now I am going. Can't you see that I already have my hand on the handle of the door? Good-bye, good-bye," I say. "You might answer me when I say good-bye twice, and stand on the point of going. I don't even ask to meet you again, for it would torment you. But tell me, why didn't you leave me in peace? What had I done to you? I didn't get in your way, now, did I? Why did you turn away from me all at once, as if you didn't know me any longer? You have plucked me now so thoroughly bare, made me even more wretched than I ever was at any time before; but, indeed, I am not insane. You know well, if you think it over, that nothing is the matter with me now. Come over, then, and give me your hand—or give me leave to go to you, will you? I won't do you any harm; I will only kneel before you, only for a minute—kneel down on the floor before you, only for a minute, may I? No, no; there, I am not to do it then, I see. You are getting afraid. I will not, I will not do it; do you hear? Lord, why do you get so terrified. I am standing quite still; I am not moving. I would have knelt down on the carpet for a moment—just there, upon that patch of red, at your feet; but you got frightened—I could see it at once in your eyes that you got frightened; that was why I stood still. I didn't move a step when I asked you might I, did I? I stood just as immovable as I stand now when I point out the place to you where I would have knelt before you, over there on the crimson rose in the carpet. I don't even point with my finger. I don't point at all; I let it be, not to frighten you. I only nod and look over at it, like this! and you know perfectly well which rose I mean, but you won't let me kneel there. You are afraid of me, and dare not come near to me. I cannot conceive how you could have the heart to call me insane. It isn't true; you don't believe it, either, any longer? It was once in the summer, a long time ago, I was mad; I worked too hard, and forgot to go to dine at the right hour, when I had too much to think about. That happened day after day. I ought to have remembered it; but I went on forgetting it—by God in Heaven, it is true! God keep me from ever coming alive from this spot if I lie. There, you can see, you do me an injustice. It was not out of need I did it; I can get credit, much credit, at Ingebret's or Gravesen's. I often, too, had a good deal of money in my pocket, and did not buy food all the same, because I forgot it. Do you hear? You don't say anything; you don't answer; you don't stir a bit from the fire; you just stand and wait for me to go...."

She came hurriedly over to me, and stretched out her hand. I looked at her, full of mistrust. Did she do it with any true heartiness, or did she only do it to get rid of me? She wound her arms round my neck; she had tears in her eyes; I only stood and looked at her. She offered her mouth; I couldn't believe in her; it was quite certain she was making a sacrifice as a means of putting an end to all this.

She said something; it sounded to me like, "I am fond of you, in spite of all." She said it very lowly and indistinctly; maybe I did not hear aright. She may not have said just those words; but she cast herself impetuously against my breast, clasped both her arms about my neck for a little while, stretched even up a bit on her toes to get a good hold, and stood so for perhaps a whole minute. I was afraid that she was forcing herself to show me this tenderness, and I only said:

"What a darling you are now!"

More I didn't say. I crushed her in my arms, stepped back, rushed to the door, and went out backwards. She remained in there behind me.

Part IV

Winter had set in—a raw, wet winter, almost without snow. A foggy, dark, and everlasting night, without a single blast of fresh wind the whole week through. The gas was lighted almost all the day in the streets, and yet people jostled one another in the fog. Every sound, the clang of the church bells, the jingling of the harness of the drosche horses, the people's voices, the beat of the hoofs, everything, sounded choked and jangling through the close air, that penetrated and muffled everything.

Week followed week, and the weather was, and remained, still the same.

And I stayed steadily down in Vaterland. I grew more and more closely bound to this inn, this lodging-house for travellers, where I had found shelter, in spite of my starving condition. My money was exhausted long since; and yet I continued to come and go in this place as if I had a right to it, and was at home there. The landlady had, as yet, said nothing; but it worried me all the same that I could not pay her. In this way three weeks went by. I had already, many days ago, taken to writing again; but I could not succeed in putting anything together that satisfied me. I had not longer any luck, although I was very painstaking, and strove early and late; no matter what I attempted, it was useless. Good fortune had flown; and I exerted myself in vain.

It was in a room on the second floor, the best guest-room, that I sat and made these attempts. I had been undisturbed up there since the first evening when I had money and was able to settle for what I got. All the time I was buoyed up by the hope of at last succeeding in getting together an article on some subject or another, so that I could pay for my room, and for whatever else I owed. That was the reason I worked on so persistently. I had, in particular, commenced a piece from which I expected great things—an allegory about a fire—a profound thought upon which I intended to expend all my energy, and bring it to the "Commander" in payment. The "Commodore" should see that he had helped a talent this time. I had no doubt but that he would eventually see that; it only was a matter of waiting till the spirit moved me; and why shouldn't the spirit move me? Why should it not come over me even now, at a very early date? There was no longer anything the matter with me. My landlady gave me a little food every day, some bread and butter, mornings and evenings, and my nervousness had almost flown. I no longer used cloths round my hands when I wrote; and I could stare down into the street from my window on the second floor without getting giddy. I was much better in every way, and it was becoming a matter of astonishment to me that I had not already finished my allegory. I couldn't understand why it was....

But a day came when I was at last to get a clear idea of how weak I had really become; with what incapacity my dull brain acted. Namely, on this day my landlady came up to me with a reckoning which she asked me to look over. There must be something wrong in this reckoning, she said; it didn't agree with her own book; but she had not been able to find out the mistake.

I set to work to add up. My landlady sat right opposite and looked at me. I added up these score of figures first once down, and found the total right; then once up again, and arrived at the same result. I looked at the woman sitting opposite me, waiting on my words. I noticed at the same time that she was pregnant; it did not escape my attention, and yet I did not stare in any way scrutinizingly at her.

"The total is right," said I.

"No; go over each figure now," she answered. "I am sure it can't be so much; I am positive of it."

And I commenced to check each line—2 loaves at 2 1/2d., 1 lamp chimney, 3d., soap, 4d., butter, 5d.... It did not require any particularly shrewd head to run up these rows of figures—this little huckster account in which nothing very complex occurred. I tried honestly to find the error that the woman spoke about, but couldn't succeed. After I had muddled about with these figures for some minutes I felt that, unfortunately, everything commenced to dance about in my head; I could no longer distinguish debit or credit; I mixed the whole thing up. Finally, I came to a dead stop at the following entry—"3. 5/16ths of a pound of cheese at 9d." My brain failed me completely; I stared stupidly down at the cheese, and got no farther.

"It is really too confoundedly crabbed writing," I exclaimed in despair. "Why, God bless me, here is 5/16ths of a pound of cheese entered—ha, ha! did any one ever hear the like? Yes, look here; you can see for yourself."

"Yes," she said; "it is often put down like that; it is a kind of Dutch cheese. Yes, that is all right—five-sixteenths is in this case five ounces."

"Yes, yes; I understand that well enough," I interrupted, although in truth I understood nothing more whatever.

I tried once more to get this little account right, that I could have totted up in a second some months ago. I sweated fearfully, and thought over these enigmatical figures with all my might, and I blinked my eyes reflectingly, as if I was studying this matter sharply, but I had to give it up. These five ounces of cheese finished me completely; it was as if something snapped within my forehead. But yet, to give the impression that I still worked out my calculation, I moved my lips and muttered a number aloud, all the while sliding farther and farther down the reckoning as if I were steadily coming to a result. She sat and waited. At last I said:

"Well, now, I have gone through it from first to last, and there is no mistake, as far as I can see."

"Isn't there?" replied the woman, "isn't there really?" But I saw well that she did not believe me, and she seemed all at once to throw a dash of contempt into her words, a slightly careless tone that I had never heard from her before. She remarked that perhaps I was not accustomed to reckon in sixteenths; she mentioned also that she must only apply to some one who had a knowledge of sixteenths, to get the account properly revised. She said all this, not in any hurtful way to make me feel ashamed, but thoughtfully and seriously. When she got as far as the door, she said, without looking at me:

"Excuse me for taking up your time then."

Off she went.

A moment after, the door opened again, and she re-entered. She could hardly have gone much farther than the stairs before she had turned back.

"That's true," said she; "you mustn't take it amiss; but there is a little owing to me from you now, isn't there? Wasn't it three weeks yesterday since you came?" Yes, I thought it was. "It isn't so easy to keep things going with such a big family, so that I can't give lodging on credit, more's the...."

I stopped her. "I am working at an article that I think I told you about before," said I, "and as soon as ever that is finished, you shall have your money; you can make yourself quite easy...."

"Yes; but you'll never get that article finished, though."

"Do you think that? Maybe the spirit will move me tomorrow, or perhaps already, tonight; it isn't at all impossible but that it may move me some time tonight, and then my article will be completed in a quarter of an hour at the outside. You see, it isn't with my work as with other people's; I can't sit down and get a certain amount finished in a day. I have just to wait for the right moment, and no one can tell the day or hour when the spirit may move one—it must have its own time...."

My landlady went, but her confidence in me was evidently much shaken.

As soon as I was left alone I jumped up and tore my hair in despair. No, in spite of all, there was really no salvation for me—no salvation! My brain was bankrupt! Had I then really turned into a complete dolt since I could not even add up the price of a piece of Dutch cheese? But could it be possible I had lost my senses when I could stand and put such questions to myself? Had not I, into the bargain, right in the midst of my efforts with the reckoning, made the lucid observation that my landlady was in the family way? I had no reason for knowing it, no one had told me anything about it, neither had it occurred to me gratuitously. I sat and saw it with my own eyes, and I understood it at once, right at a despairing moment where I sat and added up sixteenths. How could I explain this to myself?

I went to the window and gazed out; it looked out into Vognmandsgade. Some children were playing down on the pavement; poorly dressed children in the middle of a poor street. They tossed an empty bottle between them and screamed shrilly. A load of furniture rolled slowly by; it must belong to some dislodged family, forced to change residence between "flitting time."[6] This struck me at once. Bed-clothes and furniture were heaped on the float, moth-eaten beds and chests of drawers, red-painted chairs with three legs, mats, old iron, and tin-ware. A little girl—a mere child, a downright ugly youngster, with a running cold in her nose—sat up on top of the load, and held fast with her poor little blue hands in order not to tumble off. She sat on a heap of frightfully stained mattresses, that children must have lain on, and looked down at the urchins who were tossing the empty bottle to one

[6] In Norway, 14th of March and October.

another....

I stood gazing at all this; I had no difficulty in apprehending everything that passed before me. Whilst I stood there at the window and observed this, I could hear my landlady's servant singing in the kitchen right alongside of my room. I knew the air she was singing, and I listened to hear if she would sing false, and I said to myself that an idiot could not have done all this.

I was, God be praised, all right in my senses as any man.

Suddenly, I saw two of the children down in the street fire up and begin to abuse one another. Two little boys; I recognized one of them; he was my landlady's son. I open the window to hear what they are saying to one another, and immediately a flock of children crowded together under my window, and looked wistfully up. What did they expect? That something would be thrown down? Withered flowers, bones, cigar ends, or one thing or another, that they could amuse themselves with? They looked up with their frost-pinched faces and unspeakably wistful eyes. In the meantime, the two small foes continued to revile one another.

Words like great buzzing noxious insects swarm out of their childish mouths; frightful nicknames, thieves' slang, sailors' oaths, that they perhaps had learnt down on the wharf; and they are both so engaged that they do not notice my landlady, who rushes out to see what is going on.

"Yes," explains her son, "he catched me by the throat; I couldn't breaths for ever so long," and turning upon the little man who is the cause of the quarrel, and who is standing grinning maliciously at him, he gets perfectly furious, and yells, "Go to hell, Chaldean ass that you are! To think such vermin as you should catch folk by the throat. I will, may the Lord...."

And the mother, this pregnant woman, who dominates the whole street with her size, answers the ten-year-old child, as she seizes him by the arm and tries to drag him in:

"Sh—sh. Hold your jaw! I just like to hear the way you swear, too, as if you had been in a brothel for years. Now, in with you."

"No, I won't."

"Yes, you will."

"No, I won't."

I stand up in the window and see that the mother's temper is rising; this disagreeable scene excites me frightfully. I can't endure it any longer. I call down to the boy to come up to me for a minute; I call twice, just to distract them—to change the scene. The last time I call very loudly, and the mother turns round flurriedly and looks up at me. She regains her self-possession at once, looks insolently at me, nay, downright maliciously, and enters the house with a chiding remark to her offspring. She talks loudly, so that I may hear it, and says to him,

"Fie, you ought to be ashamed of yourself to let people see how naughty you are."

Of all this that I stood there and observed not one thing, not even one little accessory detail, was lost on me; my attention was acutely keen; I absorbed carefully every little thing as I stood and thought out my own thought, about each thing according as it occurred. So it was impossible that there could be anything the matter with my brain. How could there, in this case, be anything the matter with it?

Listen; do you know what, said I all at once to myself, that you have been worrying yourself long enough about your brain, giving yourself no end of worry in this matter? Now, there must be an end to this tomfoolery. Is it a sign of insanity to notice and apprehend everything as accurately as you do? You make me almost laugh at you, I reply. To my mind it is not without its humorous side, if I am any judge of such a case. Why, it happens to every man that he once in a way sticks fast, and that, too, just with the simplest question. It is of no significance, it is often a pure accident. As I have remarked before, I am on the point of having a good laugh at your expense. As far as that huckster account is concerned, that paltry five-sixteenths of beggar-man's cheese, I can happily dub it so. Ha, ha!— a cheese with cloves and pepper in it; upon my word, a cheese in which, to put the matter plainly, one could breed maggots. As far as that ridiculous cheese is concerned, it might happen to the cleverest fellow in the world to be puzzled over it! Why, the smell of the cheese was enough to finish a man; ... and I made the greatest fun of this and all other Dutch cheeses.... No; set me to reckon up something really eatable, said I—set me, if you like, at five-sixteenths of good dairy butter. That is another matter.

I laughed feverishly at my own whim, and found it peculiarly diverting. There was positively no longer anything the matter with me. I was in good form—was, so to say, still in the best of form; I had a level head, nothing was wanting there, God be praised and thanked! My mirth rose in measure as I paced the floor and communed with myself. I laughed aloud, and felt amazingly glad. Besides, it really seemed, too, as if I only needed this little happy hour, this moment of airy rapture, without a care on any side, to get my head into working order once more.

I seated myself at the table, and set to work at my allegory; it progressed swimmingly, better than it had done for a long time; not very fast, 'tis true, but it seemed to me that what I did was altogether first-rate. I worked, too, for the space of an hour without getting tired.

I am sitting working at a most crucial point in this Allegory of a Conflagration in a Bookshop. It appears to me so momentous a point, that all the rest I have written counted as nothing in comparison. I was, namely, just about to weave in, in a downright profound way, this thought. It was not books that were burning, it was brains, human brains; and I intended to make a perfect Bartholomew's night of these burning brains.

Suddenly my door was flung open with a jerk and in much haste; my landlady came sailing in. She came straight over to the middle of the room, she did not even pause on the threshold.

I gave a little hoarse cry; it was just as if I had received a blow.

"What?" said she, "I thought you said something. We have got a traveller, and we must have this room for him. You will have to sleep downstairs with us tonight. Yes; you can have a bed to yourself there too." And before she got my answer, she began, without further ceremony, to bundle my papers together on the table, and put the whole of them into a state of dire confusion.

My happy mood was blown to the winds; I stood up at once, in anger and despair. I let her tidy the table, and said nothing, never uttered a syllable. She thrust all the papers into my hand.

There was nothing else for me to do. I was forced to leave the room. And so this precious moment was spoilt also. I met the new traveller already on the stairs; a young man with great blue anchors tattooed on the backs of his hands. A quay porter followed him, bearing a sea-chest on his shoulders. He was evidently a sailor, a casual traveller for the night; he would therefore not occupy my room for any lengthened period. Perhaps, too, I might be lucky tomorrow when the man had left, and have one of my moments again; I only needed an inspiration for five minutes, and my essay on the conflagration would be completed. Well, I should have to submit to fate.

I had not been inside the family rooms before, this one common room in which they all lived, both day and night—the husband, wife, wife's father, and four children. The servant lived in the kitchen, where she also slept at night. I approached the door with much repugnance, and knocked. No one answered, yet I heard voices inside.

The husband did not speak as I stepped in, did not acknowledge my nod even, merely glanced at me carelessly, as if I were no concern of his. Besides, he was sitting playing cards with a person I had seen down on the quays, with the by-name of "Pane o' glass." An infant lay and prattled to itself over in the bed, and an old man, the landlady's father, sat doubled together on a settle-bed, and bent his head down Over his hands as if his chest or stomach pained him. His hair was almost white, and he looked in his crouching position like a poke-necked reptile that sat cocking its ears at something.

"I come, worse luck, to beg for house-room down here tonight," I said to the man.

"Did my wife say so?" he inquired.

"Yes; a new lodger came to my room."

To this the man made no reply, but proceeded to finger the cards.

There this man sat, day after day, and played cards with anybody who happened to come in—played for nothing, only just to kill time, and have something in hand. He never did anything else, only moved just as much as his lazy limbs felt inclined, whilst his wife bustled up and down stairs, was occupied on all sides, and took care to draw customers to the house. She had put herself in connection with quay-porters and dock-men, to whom she paid a certain sum for every new lodger they brought her, and she often gave them, in addition, a shelter for the night. This time it was "Pane o' glass" that had just brought along the new lodger.

A couple of the children came in—two little girls, with thin, freckled, gutter-snipe faces; their clothes were positively wretched. A while after the landlady herself entered. I asked her where she intended to put me up for the night, and she replied that I could lie in here together with the others, or out in the ante-room on the sofa, as I thought fit. Whilst she answered me she fussed about the room and busied herself with different things that she set in order, and she never once looked at me.

My spirits were crushed by her reply.

I stood down near the door, and made myself small, tried to make it appear as if I were quite content all the same to change my room for another for one night's sake. I put on a friendly face on purpose not to irritate her and perhaps be hustled right out of the house.

"Ah, yes," I said, "there is sure to be some way I . . .," and then held my tongue.

She still bustled about the room.

"For that matter, I may as well just tell you that I can't afford to give people credit for their board and lodging," said she, "and I told you that before, too."

"Yes; but, my dear woman, it is only for these few days, until I get my article finished," I answered, "and I will willingly give you an extra five shillings—willingly."

But she had evidently no faith in my article, I could see that; and I could not afford to be proud, and leave the house, just for a slight mortification; I knew what awaited me if I went out.

A few days passed over.

I still associated with the family below, for it was too cold in the ante-room where there was no stove. I slept, too, at night on the floor of the room.

The strange sailor continued to lodge in my room, and did not seem like moving very quickly. At noon, too, my landlady came in and related how he had paid her a month in advance, and besides, he was going to take his first-mate's examination before leaving, that was why he was staying in town. I stood and listened to this, and understood that my room was lost to me for ever.

I went out to the ante-room, and sat down. If I were lucky enough to get anything written, it would have perforce to be here where it was quiet. It was no longer the allegory that occupied me; I had got a new idea, a perfectly splendid plot; I would compose a one-act drama—"The Sign of the Cross." Subject taken from the Middle Ages. I had especially thought out everything in connection with the principal characters: a magnificently fanatical harlot who had sinned in the temple, not from weakness or desire, but for hate against heaven; sinner right at the foot of the altar, with the altar-cloth under her head, just out of delicious contempt for heaven.

I grew more and more obsessed by this creation as the hours went on. She stood at last, palpably, vividly embodied before my eyes, and was exactly as I wished her to appear. Her body was to be deformed and repulsive, tall, very lean, and rather dark; and when she walked, her long limbs should gleam through her draperies at every stride she took. She was also to have large outstanding ears. Curtly, she was nothing for the eye to dwell upon, barely endurable to look at. What interested me in her was her wonderful shamelessness, the desperately full measure of calculated sin which she had committed. She really occupied me too much, my brain was absolutely inflated by this singular monstrosity of a creature, and I worked for two hours, without a pause, at my drama. When I had finished half-a score of pages, perhaps twelve, often with much effort, at times with long intervals, in which I wrote in vain and had to tear the page in two, I had become tired, quite stiff with cold and fatigue, and I arose and went out into the street. For the last half-hour, too, I had been disturbed by the crying of the children inside the family room, so that I could not, in any case, have written any more just then. So I took a long time up over Drammensveien, and stayed away till the evening, pondering incessantly, as I walked along, as to how I would continue my drama. Before I came home in the evening of this day, the following happened:

I stood outside a shoemaker's shop far down in Carl Johann Street, almost at the railway square. God knows why I stood just outside this shoemaker's shop. I looked into the window as I stood there, but did not, by the way, remember that I needed shoes then; my thoughts were far away in other parts of the world. A swarm of people talking together passed behind my back, and I heard nothing of what was said. Then a voice greeted me loudly:

"Good-evening."

It was "Missy" who bade me good-evening! I answered at random, I looked at him, too, for a while, before I recognized him.

"Well, how are you getting along?" he inquired.

"Oh, always well ... as usual."

"By the way, tell me," said he, "are you, then, still with Christie?"

"Christie?"

"I thought you once said you were book-keeper at Christie's?"

"Ah, yes. No; that is done with. It was impossible to get along with that fellow; that came to an end very quickly of its own accord."

"Why so?"

"Well, I happened to make a mis-entry one day, and so—"

"A false entry, eh?"

False entry! There stood "Missy," and asked me straight in the face if I had done this thing. He even asked eagerly, and evidently with much interest. I looked at him, felt deeply insulted, and made no reply.

"Yes, well, Lord! that might happen to the best fellow," he said, as if to console me. He still believed I had made a false entry designedly.

"What is it that, 'Yes, well, Lord! indeed might happen to the best fellow'?" I inquired. "To do that. Listen, my good man. Do you stand there and really believe that I could for a moment be guilty of such a mean trick as that? I!"

"But, my dear fellow, I thought I heard you distinctly say that."

"No; I said that I had made a mis-entry once, a bagatelle; if you want to know, a false date on a letter, a single stroke of the pen wrong—that was my whole crime. No, God be praised, I can tell right from wrong yet a while. How would it fare with me if I were, into the bargain, to sully my honour? It is simply my sense of honour that keeps me afloat now. But it is strong enough too; at least, it has kept me up to date."

I threw back my head, turned away from "Missy," and looked down the street. My eyes rested on a red dress that came towards us; on a woman at a man's side. If I had not had this conversation with "Missy," I would not have been hurt by his coarse suspicion, and I would not have given this toss of my head, as I turned away in offence; and so perhaps this red dress would have passed me without my having noticed it. And at bottom what did it concern me? What was it to me if it were the dress of the Hon. Miss Nagel, the lady-in-waiting? "Missy" stood and talked, and tried to make good his mistake again. I did not listen to him at all; I stood the whole time and stared at the red dress that was coming nearer up the street, and a stir thrilled through my breast, a gliding delicate dart. I whispered in thought without moving my lips:

"Ylajali!"

Now "Missy" turned round also and noticed the two—the lady and the man with her,—raised his hat to them, and followed them with his eyes. I did not raise my hat, or perhaps I did unconsciously. The red dress glided up Carl Johann, and disappeared.

"Who was it was with her?" asked "Missy."

"The Duke, didn't you see? The so-called 'Duke.' Did you know the lady?"

"Yes, in a sort of way. Didn't you know her?"

"No," I replied.

"It appears to me you saluted profoundly enough."

"Did I?"

"Ha, ha! perhaps you didn't," said "Missy." "Well, that is odd. Why, it was only at you she looked, too, the whole time."

"When did you get to know her?" I asked. He did not really know her. It dated from an evening in autumn. It was late; they were three jovial souls together, they came out late from the Grand, and met this being going along alone past Cammermeyer's, and they addressed her. At first she answered rebuffingly; but one of the jovial spirits, a man who neither feared fire nor water, asked her right to her face if he might not have the civilized enjoyment of accompanying her home? He would, by the Lord, not hurt a hair on her head, as the saying goes—only go with her to her door, reassure himself that she reached home in safety, otherwise he could not rest all night. He talked incessantly as they went along, hit upon one thing or another, dubbed himself Waldemar Atterdag, and represented himself as a photographer. At last she was obliged to laugh at this merry soul who refused to be rebuffed by her coldness, and it finally ended by his going with her.

"Indeed, did it? and what came of it?" I inquired; and I held my breath for his reply.

"Came of it? Oh, stop there; there is the lady in question."

We both kept silent a moment, both "Missy" and I.

"Well, I'm hanged, was that 'the Duke'? So that's what he looks like," he added, reflectively. "Well, if she is in contact with that fellow; well, then, I wouldn't like to answer for her."

I still kept silent. Yes, of course "the Duke" would make the pace with her. Well, what odds? How did it concern me? I bade her good-day with all her wiles: a good-day I bade her; and I tried to console myself by thinking the worst thoughts about her; took a downright pleasure in dragging her through the mire. It only annoyed me to think that I had doffed my hat to the pair, if I really had done so. Why should I raise my hat to such people? I did not care for her any longer, certainly not; she was no longer in the very slightest degree lovely to me; she had fallen off. Ah, the devil knows how soiled I found her! It might easily have been the case that it was only me she looked at; I was not in the least astounded at that; it might be regret that began to stir in her. But that was no reason for me to go and lower myself and salute, like a fool, especially when she had become so seriously besmirched of late. "The Duke" was welcome to her; I wish him joy! The day might come when I would just take into my head to pass her haughtily by without glancing once towards her. Ay, it might happen that I would venture to do this, even if she were to gaze straight into my eyes, and have a blood-red gown on into the bargain. It might very easily happen!

Ha, ha! that would be a triumph. If I knew myself aright, I was quite capable of completing my drama during the course of the night, and, before eight days had flown, I would have brought this young woman to her knees—with all her charms, ha, ha! with all her charms....

"Good-bye," I muttered, shortly; but "Missy" held me back. He queried:

"But what do you do all day now?"

"Do? I write, naturally. What else should I do? Is it not that I live by? For the moment, I am working at a great drama, 'The Sign of the Cross.' Theme taken from the Middle Ages."

"By Jove!" exclaimed "Missy," seriously. "Well, if you succeed with that, why...."

"I have no great anxiety on that score," I replied. "In eight days' time or so, I think you and all the folks will have heard a little more of me."

With that I left him.

When I got home I applied at once to my landlady, and requested a lamp. It was of the utmost importance to me to get this lamp; I would not go to bed tonight; my drama was raging in my brain, and I hoped so surely to be able to write a good portion of it before morning. I put forward my request very humbly to her, as I had noticed that she made a dissatisfied face on my re-entering the sitting-room. I said that I had almost completed a remarkable drama, only a couple of scenes were wanting; and I hinted that it might be produced in some theatre or another, in no time. If she would only just render me this great service now....

But madam had no lamp. She considered a bit, but could not call to mind that she had a lamp in any place. If I liked to wait until twelve o'clock, I might perhaps get the kitchen lamp. Why didn't I buy myself a candle?

I held my tongue. I hadn't a farthing to buy a candle, and knew that right well. Of course I was foiled again! The servant-girl sat inside with us— simply sat in the sitting-room, and was not in the kitchen at all; so that the lamp up there was not even lit. And I stood and thought over this, but said no more. Suddenly the girl remarked to me:

"I thought I saw you come out of the palace a while ago; were you at a dinner party?" and she laughed loudly at this jest.

I sat down, took out my papers, and attempted to write something here, in the meantime. I held the paper on my knees, and gazed persistently at the floor to avoid being distracted by anything; but it helped not a whit; nothing helped me; I got no farther. The landlady's two little girls came in and made a row with the cat—a queer, sick cat that had scarcely a hair on it; they blew into its eyes until water sprang out of them and trickled down its nose. The landlord and a couple of others sat at a table and played cent et un. The wife alone was busy as ever, and sat and sewed at some garment. She saw well that I could not write anything in the midst of all this disturbance; but she troubled herself no more about me; she even smiled when the servant-girl asked me if I had been out to dine. The whole household had become hostile towards me. It was as if I had only needed disgrace of being obliged to resign my room to a stranger to be treated as a man of no account. Even the servant, a little, brown-eyed, street-wench, with a big fringe over her forehead, and a perfectly flat bosom, poked fun at me in the evening when I got my ration of bread and butter. She inquired perpetually where, then, was I in the habit of dining, as she had never seen me picking my teeth outside the Grand? It was clear that she was aware of my wretched circumstances, and took a pleasure in letting me know of it.

I fall suddenly into thought over all this, and am not able to find a solitary speech for my drama. Time upon time I seek in vain; a strange buzzing begins inside my head, and I give it up. I thrust the papers into my pocket, and look up. The girl is sitting straight opposite me. I look at her—look at her narrow back and drooping shoulders, that are not yet fully developed. What business was it of hers to fly at me? Even supposing I did come out of the palace, what then? Did it harm her in any way? She had laughed insolently in the past few days at me, when I was a bit awkward and stumbled on the stairs, or caught fast on a nail and tore my coat. It was not later than yesterday that she gathered up my rough copy, that I had thrown aside in the ante-room—stolen these rejected fragments of my drama, and read them aloud in the room here; made fun of them in every one's hearing, just to amuse herself at my expense. I had never molested her in any way, and could not recall that I had ever asked her to do me a service. On the contrary, I made up my bed on the floor in the ante-room myself, in order not to give her any trouble with it. She made fun of me, too, because my hair fell out. Hair lay and floated about in the basin I washed in the mornings, and she made merry over it. Then my shoes, too, had grown rather shabby of late, particularly the one that had been run over by the bread-van, and she found subject for jesting in them. "God bless you and your shoes!" said she, looking at them; "they are as wide as a dog's house." And she was right; they were trodden out. But then I couldn't procure myself any others just at present.

Whilst I sit and call all this to mind, and marvel over the evident malice of the servant, the little girls have begun to tease the old man over in the bed; they are jumping around him, fully bent on this diversion. They both found a straw, which they poked into his ears. I looked on at this for a while, and refrained from interfering. The old fellow did not move a finger to defend himself; he only looked at his tormentors with furious eyes each time they prodded him, and jerked his head to escape when the straws were already in his ears. I got more and more irritated at this sight, and could not keep my eyes away from it. The father looked up from his cards, and laughed at the youngsters; he also drew the attention of his comrades at play to what was going on. Why didn't the old fellow move? Why didn't he fling the children aside with his arms? I took a stride, and approached the bed.

"Let them alone! let them alone! he is paralysed," called the landlord.

And out of fear to be shown the door for the night, simply out of fear of rousing the man's displeasure by interfering with this scene, I stepped back silently to my old place and kept myself quiet. Why should I risk my lodging and my portion of bread and butter by poking my nose into the family squabbles? No idiotic pranks for the sake of a half-dying old man, and I stood and felt as delightfully hard as a flint.

The little urchins did not cease their plaguing; it amused them that the old chap could not hold his head quiet, and they aimed at his eyes and nostrils. He stared at them with a ludicrous expression; he said nothing, and could not stir his arms. Suddenly he raised the upper part of his body a little and spat in the face of one of the little girls, drew himself up again and spat at the other, but did not reach her. I stood and looked on, saw that the landlord flung the cards on the table at which he sat, and sprang over towards the bed. His face was flushed, and he shouted:

"Will you sit and spit right into people's eyes, you old boar?"

"But, good Lord, he got no peace from them!" I cried, beside myself.

But all the time I stood in fear of being turned out, and I certainly did not utter my protest with any particular force; I only trembled over my whole body with irritation. He turned towards me, and said:

"Eh, listen to him, then. What the devil is it to you? You just keep your tongue in your jaw, you—just mark what I tell you, 'twill serve you best."

But now the wife's voice made itself heard, and the house was filled with scolding and railing.

"May God help me, but I think you are mad or possessed, the whole pack of you!" she shrieked. "If you want to stay in here you'll have to be quiet, both of you! Humph! it isn't enough that one is to keep open house and food for vermin, but one is to have sparring and rowing and the devil's own to-do in the sitting-room as well. But I won't have any more of it, not if I know it. Sh—h! Hold your tongues, you brats there, and wipe your noses, too; if you don't, I'll come and do it. I never saw the like of such people. Here they walk in out of the street, without even a penny to buy flea-powder, and begin to kick up rows in the middle of the night and quarrel with the people who own the house, I don't mean to have any more of it, do you understand that? and you can go your way, every one who doesn't belong home here. I am going to have peace in my own quarters, I am."

I said nothing, I never opened my mouth once. I sat down again next the door and listened to the noise. They all screamed together, even the children, and the girl who wanted to explain how the whole disturbance commenced. If I only kept quiet it would all blow over sometime; it would surely not come to the worst if I only did not utter a word; and what word after all could I have to say? Was it not perhaps winter outside, and far advanced into the night, besides? Was that a time to strike a blow, and show one could hold one's own? No folly now!... So I sat still and made no attempt to leave the house; I never even blushed at keeping silent, never felt ashamed, although I had almost been shown the door. I stared coolly, case-hardened, at the wall where Christ hung in an oleograph, and held my tongue obstinately during all the landlady's attack.

"Well, if it is me you want to get quit of, ma'am, there will be nothing in the way as far as I am concerned," said one of the card-players as he stood up. The other card-players rose as well.

"No, I didn't mean you—nor you either," replied the landlady to them. "If there's any need to, I will show well enough who I mean, if there's the least need to, if I know myself rightly. Oh, it will be shown quick enough who it is...."

She talked with pauses, gave me these thrusts at short intervals, and spun it out to make it clearer and clearer that it was me she meant. "Quiet," said I to myself; "only keep quiet!" She had not asked me to go—not expressly, not in plain words. Just no putting on side on my part—no untimely pride! Brave it out!... That was really most singular green hair on that Christ in the oleograph. It was not too unlike green grass, or expressed with exquisite exactitude thick meadow grass. Ha! a perfectly correct remark—unusually thick meadow grass.... A train of fleeting ideas darts at this moment through my head. From green grass to the text, Each life is like unto grass that is kindled; from that to the Day of Judgment, when all will be consumed; then a little detour down to the earthquake in Lisbon, about which something floated before me in reference to a brass Spanish spittoon and an ebony pen handle that I had seen down at Ylajali's. Ah, yes, all was transitory, just like grass that was kindled. It all ended in four planks and a winding-sheet. "Winding-sheets to be had from Miss Andersen's, on the right of the door...." And all this was tossed about in my head during the despairing moment when my landlady was about to thrust me from her door.

"He doesn't hear," she yelled. "I tell you, you'll quit this house. Now you know it. I believe God blast me, that the man is mad, I do! Now, out you go, on the blessed spot, and so no more chat about it."

I looked towards the door, not in order to leave—no, certainly not in order to leave. An audacious notion seized me—if there had been a key in the door, I would have turned it and locked myself in along with the rest to escape going. I had a perfectly hysterical dread of going out into the streets again.

But there was no key in the door.

Then, suddenly my landlord's voice mingled with that of his wife, and I stood still with amazement. The same man who had threatened me a while ago took my part, strangely enough now. He said:

"No, it won't do to turn folk out at night; do you know one can be punished for doing that?"

"I didn't know if there was a punishment for that; I couldn't say, but perhaps it was so," and the wife bethought herself quickly, grew quiet, and spoke no more.

She placed two pieces of bread and butter before me for supper, but I did not touch them, just out of gratitude to the man; so I pretended that I had had a little food in town.

When at length I took myself off to the anteroom to go to bed, she came out after me, stopped on the threshold, and said loudly, whilst her unsightly figure seemed to strut out towards me:

"But this is the last night you sleep here, so now you know it."

"Yes, yes," I replied.

There would perhaps be some way of finding a shelter tomorrow, if I tried hard for it. I would surely be able to find some hiding-place. For the time being I would rejoice that I was not obliged to go out tonight.

I slept till between five and six in the morning—it was not yet light when I awoke—but all the same I got up at once. I had lain in all my clothes on account of the cold, and had no dressing to do. When I had drunk a little cold water and opened the door quietly, I went out directly, for I was afraid to face my landlady again.

A couple of policemen who had been on watch all night were the only living beings I saw in the street. A while after, some men began to extinguish the lamps. I wandered about without aim or end, reached Kirkegaden and the road down towards the fortress. Cold and still sleepy, weak in the knees and back after my long walk, and very hungry, I sat down on a seat and dozed for a long time. For three weeks I had lived exclusively on the bread and butter that my landlady had given me morning and evening. Now it was twenty-four hours since I had had my last meal. Hunger began to gnaw badly at me again; I must seek a help for it right quickly. With this thought I fell asleep again upon the seat....

I was aroused by the sound of people speaking near me, and when I had collected myself a little I saw that it was broad day, and that every one was up and about. I got up and walked away. The sun burst over the heights, the sky was pale and tender, and in my delight over the lovely morning, after the many dark gloomy weeks, I forgot all cares, and it seemed to me as if I had fared worse on other occasions. I clapped myself on the chest and sang a little snatch for myself. My voice sounded so wretched, downright exhausted it sounded, and I moved myself to tears with it. This magnificent day, the white heavens swimming in light, had far too mighty an effect upon me, and I burst into loud weeping.

"What is the matter with you?" inquired a man. I did not answer, but hurried away, hiding my face from all men. I reached the bridge. A large barque with the Russian flag lay and discharged coal. I read her name, Copégoro, on her side. It distracted me for a time to watch what took place on board this foreign ship. She must be almost discharged; she lay with IX foot visible on her side, in spite of all the ballast she had already taken in, and there was a hollow boom through the whole ship whenever the coal-heavers stamped on the deck with their heavy boots.

The sun, the light, and the salt breath from the sea, all this busy, merry life pulled me together a bit, and caused my blood to run lustily. Suddenly it entered my head that I could work at a few scenes of my drama whilst I sat here, and I took my papers out of my pocket.

I tried to place a speech into a monk's mouth—a speech that ought to swell with pride and intolerance, but it was of no use; so I skipped over the monk and tried to work out an oration—the Deemster's oration to the violator of the Temple,—and I wrote half-a-page of this oration, upon which I stopped. The right local colour would not tinge my words, the bustle about me, the shanties, the noise of the gangways, and the ceaseless rattle of the iron chains, fitted in so little with the atmosphere of the musty air of the dim Middle Ages, that was to envelop my drama as with a mist.

I bundled my papers together and got up.

All the same, I got into a happy vein—a grand vein,—and I felt convinced that I could effect something if all went well.

If I only had a place to go to. I thought over it—stopped right there in the street and pondered, but I could not bring to mind a single quiet spot in the town where I could seat myself for an hour. There was no other way open; I would have to go back to the lodging-house in Vaterland. I shrank at the thought of it, and I told myself all the while that it would not do. I went ahead all the same, and approached nearer and nearer to the forbidden spot. Of course it was wretched. I admitted to myself that it was degrading—downright degrading, but there was no help for it. I was not in the least proud; I dared make the assertion roundly, that I was one of the least arrogant beings up to date. I went ahead.

I pulled up at the door and weighed it over once more. Yes, no matter what the result was, I would have to dare it. After all said and done, what a bagatelle to make such a fuss about. For the first it was only a matter of a couple of hours; for the second, the Lord forbid that I should ever seek refuge in such a house again. I entered the yard. Even whilst I was crossing the uneven stones I was irresolute, and almost turned round at the very door. I clenched my teeth. No! no pride! At the worst I could excuse myself by saying I had come to say good-bye, to make a proper adieu, and come to a clear understanding about my debt to the house....

I took forth my papers once more, and determined to thrust all irrelevant impressions aside. I had left off right in the middle of a sentence in the inquisitor's address—"Thus dictate God and the law to me, thus dictates also the counsel of my wise men, thus dictate I and my own conscience...." I looked out of the window to think over what his conscience should dictate to him. A little row reached me from the room inside. Well, it was no affair of mine anyway; it was entirely and totally indifferent to me what noise arose. Why the devil should I sit thinking about it? Keep quiet now! "Thus dictate I and my own conscience...." But everything conspired against me. Outside in the street, something was taking place that disturbed me. A little lad sat and amused himself in the sun on the opposite side of the pavement. He was happy and in fear of no danger—just sat and knotted together a lot of paper streamers, and injuring no one. Suddenly he jumps up and begins to curse; he goes backwards to the middle of the street and catches sight of a man, a grown-up man, with a red beard, who is leaning out of an open window in the second storey, and who spat down on his head. The little chap cried with rage, and swore impatiently up at the window; and the man laughed in his face. Perhaps five minutes passed in this way. I turned aside to avoid seeing the little lad's tears.

"Thus dictate I and my own conscience...." I found it impossible to get any farther. At last everything began to get confused; it seemed to me that even that which I had already written was unfit to use, ay, that the whole idea was contemptible rubbish. How could one possibly talk of conscience in the Middle Ages? Conscience was first invented by Dancing-master Shakespeare, consequently my whole address was wrong. Was there, then, nothing of value in these pages? I ran through them anew, and solved my doubt at once. I discovered grand pieces—downright lengthy pieces of remarkable merit—and once again the intoxicating desire to set to work again darted through my breast—the desire to finish my drama.

I got up and went to the door, without paying any attention to my landlord's furious signs to go out quietly; I walked out of the room firmly, and with my mind made up. I went upstairs to the second floor, and entered my former room. The man was not there, and what was to hinder me from sitting here for a moment? I would not touch one of his things. I wouldn't even once use his table; I would just seat myself on a chair near the door, and be happy. I spread the papers hurriedly out on my knees. Things went splendidly for a few minutes. Retort upon retort stood ready in my head, and I wrote uninterruptedly. I filled one page after the other, dashed ahead over stock and stone, chuckled softly in ecstasy over my happy vein, and was scarcely conscious of myself. The only sound I heard in this moment was my own merry chuckle.

A singularly happy idea had just struck me about a church bell—a church bell that was to peal out at a certain point in my drama. All was going ahead with overwhelming rapidity. Then I heard a step on the stairs. I tremble, and am almost beside myself; sit ready to bolt, timorous, watchful, full of fear at everything, and excited by hunger. I listen nervously, just hold the pencil still in my hand, and listen. I cannot write a word more. The door opens and the pair from below enter.

Even before I had time to make an excuse for what I had done, the landlady calls out, as if struck of a heap with amazement:

"Well, God bless and save us, if he isn't sitting here again!"

"Excuse me," I said, and I would have added more, but got no farther; the landlady flung open the door, as far as it would go, and shrieked:

"If you don't go out, now, may God blast me, but I'll fetch the police!"

I got up.

"I only wanted to say good-bye to you," I murmured; "and I had to wait for you. I didn't touch anything; I only just sat here on the chair...."

"Yes, yes; there was no harm in that," said the man. "What the devil does it matter? Let the man alone; he—"

By this time I had reached the end of the stairs. All at once I got furious with this fat, swollen woman, who followed close to my heels to get rid of me quickly, and I stood quiet a moment with the worst abusive epithets on my tongue ready to sling at her. But I bethought myself in time, and held my peace, if only out of gratitude to the stranger man who followed her, and would have to hear them. She trod close on my heels, railing incessantly, and my anger increased with every step I took.

We reached the yard below. I walked very slowly, still debating whether I would not have it out with her. I was at this moment completely blinded with rage, and I searched for the worst word—an expression that would strike her dead on the spot, like a kick in her stomach. A commissionaire passes me at the entrance. He touches his hat; I take no notice; he applies to her; and I hear that he inquires for me, but I do not turn round. A couple of steps outside the door he overtakes and stops me. He hands me an envelope. I tear it open, roughly and unwillingly. It contains half-a-sovereign—no note, not a word. I look at the man, and ask:

"What tomfoolery is this? Who is the letter from?"

"Oh, that I can't say!" he replies; "but it was a lady who gave it to me."

I stood still. The commissionaire left.

I put the coin into the envelope again, crumple it up, coin and envelope, wheel round and go straight towards the landlady, who is still keeping an eye on me from the doorway, and throw it in her face. I said nothing; I uttered no syllable—only noticed that she was examining the crumpled paper as I left her.... Ha! that is what one might call comporting oneself with dignity. Not to say a word, not to mention the contents, but crumple together, with perfect calmness, a large piece of money, and fling it straight in the face of one's persecutor! One might call that making one's exit with dignity. That was the way to treat such beasts I....

When I got to the corner of Tomtegaden and the railway place, the street commenced suddenly to swim around before my eyes; it buzzed vacantly in my head, and I staggered up against the wall of a house. I could simply go no farther, couldn't even straighten myself from the cramped position I was in. As I fell up against it, so I remained standing, and I felt that I was beginning to lose my senses. My insane anger had augmented this attack of exhaustion. I lifted my foot, and stamped on the pavement. I also tried several other things to try and regain my strength: I clenched my teeth, wrinkled my brows, and rolled my eyes despairingly; it helped a little. My thoughts grew more lucid. It was clear to me that I was about to succumb. I stretched out my hands, and pushed myself back from the wall. The street still danced wildly round me. I began to hiccough with rage, and I wrestled from my very inmost soul with my misery; made a right gallant effort not to sink down. It was not my intention to collapse; no, I would die standing. A dray rolls slowly by, and I notice there are potatoes in it; but out of sheer fury and stubbornness, I take it into my head to assert that they are not potatoes, but cabbages, and I swore frightful oaths that they were cabbages. I heard quite well what I was saying, and I swore this lie wittingly; repeating time after time, just to have the vicious satisfaction of perjuring myself. I got intoxicated with the thought of this matchless sin of mine. I raised three fingers in the air, and swore, with trembling lips, in the name of the Father, Son, and Holy Ghost, that they were cabbages.

Time went. I let myself sink down on the steps near me, and dried the sweat from my brow and throat, drew a couple of long breaths, and forced myself into calmness. The sun slid down; it declined towards the afternoon. I began once more to brood over my condition. My hunger was really something disgraceful, and, in a few hours more, night would be here again. The question was, to think of a remedy while there was yet time. My thoughts flew again to the lodging-house from which I had been hunted away. I could on no account return there; but yet one could not help thinking about it. Properly speaking, the woman was acting quite within her rights in turning me out. How could I expect to get lodging with any one when I could not pay for it? Besides, she had occasionally given me a little food; even yesterday evening, after I had annoyed her, she offered me some bread and butter. She offered it to me out of sheer good nature, because she knew I needed it, so I had no cause to complain. I began, even whilst I sat there on the step, to ask her pardon in my own mind for my behaviour. Particularly, I regretted bitterly that I had shown myself ungrateful to her at the last, and thrown half-a-sovereign in her face....

Half-a-sovereign! I gave a whistle. The letter the messenger brought me, where did it come from? It was only this instant I thought clearly over this, and I divined at once how the whole thing hung together. I grew sick with pain and shame. I whispered "Ylajali" a few times, with hoarse voice, and flung back my head. Was it not I who, no later than yesterday, had decided to pass her proudly by if I met her, to treat her with the greatest indifference? Instead of that, I had only aroused her compassion, and coaxed an alms from her. No, no, no; there would never be an end to my degradation! Not even in her presence could I maintain a decent position. I sank, simply sank, on all sides—every way I turned; sank to my knees, sank to my waist, dived under in ignominy, never to rise again—never! This was the climax! To accept half-a-sovereign in alms without being able to fling it back to the secret donor; scramble for half-pence whenever the chance offered, and keep them, use them for lodging money, in spite of one's intense inner aversion....

Could I not regain the half-sovereign in some way or another? To go back to the landlady and try to get it from her would be of no use. There must be some way, if I were to consider—if I were only to exert myself right well, and consider it over. It was not, in this case, great God, sufficient to consider in just an ordinary way! I must consider so that it penetrated my whole sentient being; consider and find some way to procure this half-sovereign. And I set to, to consider the answer to this problem.

It might be about four o'clock; in a few hours' time I could perhaps meet the manager of the theatre; if only I had my drama completed.

I take out my MSS. there where I am sitting, and resolve, with might and main, to finish the last few scenes. I think until I sweat, and re-read from the beginning, but make no progress. No bosh! I say—no obstinacy, now! and I write away at my drama—write down everything that strikes me, just to get finished quickly and be able to go away. I tried to persuade myself that a new supreme moment had seized me; I lied right royally to myself, deceived myself knowingly, and wrote on, as if I had no need to seek for words.

That is capital! That is really a find! whispered I, interpolatingly; only just write it down! Halt! they sound questionable; they contrast rather strongly with the speeches in the first scenes; not a trace of the Middle Ages shone through the monk's words. I break my pencil between my teeth, jump to my feet, tear my manuscript in two, tear each page in two, fling my hat down in the street and trample upon it. I am lost! I whisper to myself. Ladies and gentlemen, I am lost! I utter no more than these few words as long as I stand there, and tramp upon my hat.

A policeman is standing a few steps away, watching me. He is standing in the middle of the street, and he only pays attention to me. As I lift my head, our eyes meet. Maybe he has been standing there for a long time watching me. I pick up my hat, put it on, and go over to him.

"Do you know what time it is?" I ask. He pauses a bit as he hauls out his watch, and never takes his eyes off me the whole time.

"About four," he replies.

"Accurately," I say, "about four, perfectly accurate. You know your business, and I'll bear you in mind." Thereupon I left him. He looked utterly amazed at me, stood and looked at me, with gaping mouth, still holding his watch in his hand.

When I got in front of the Royal Hotel I turned and looked back. He was still standing in the same position, following me with his eyes.

Ha, ha! That is the way to treat brutes! With the most refined effrontery! That impresses the brutes—puts the fear of God into them.... I was peculiarly satisfied with myself, and began to sing a little strain. Every nerve was tense with excitement. Without feeling any more pain, without even being conscious of discomfort of any kind, I walked, light as a feather, across the whole market, turned round at the stalls, and came to a halt—sat down on a bench near Our Saviour's Church. Might it not just as well be a matter of indifference whether I returned the half-sovereign or not? When once I received it, it was mine; and there was evidently no want where it came from. Besides, I was obliged to take it when it was sent expressly to me; there could be no object in letting the messenger keep it. It wouldn't do, either, to send it back—a whole half-sovereign that had been sent to me. So there was positively no help for it.

I tried to watch the bustle about me in the market, and distract myself with indifferent things, but I did not succeed; the half-sovereign still busied my thoughts. At last I clenched my fists and got angry. It would hurt her if I were to send it back. Why, then, should I do so? Always ready to consider myself too good for everything—to toss my head and say, No, thanks! I saw now what it led to. I was out in the street again. Even when I had the opportunity I couldn't keep my good warm lodging. No; I must needs be proud, jump up at the first word, and show I wasn't the man to stand trifling, chuck half-sovereigns right and left, and go my way.... I took myself sharply to task for having left my lodging and brought myself into the most distressful circumstances.

As for the rest, I consigned the whole affair to the keeping of the yellowest of devils. I hadn't begged for the half-sovereign, and I had barely had it in my hand, but gave it away at once—paid it away to utterly strange people whom I would never see again. That was the sort of man I was; I always paid out to the last doit whatever I owed. If I knew Ylajali aright, neither did she regret that she had sent me the money, therefore why did I sit there working myself into a rage? To put it plainly, the least she could do was to send me half-a-sovereign now and then. The poor girl was indeed in love with me—ha! perhaps even fatally in love with me; ... and I sat and puffed myself up with this notion. There was no doubt that she was in love with me, the poor girl.

It struck five o'clock! Again I sank under the weight of my prolonged nervous excitement. The hollow whirring in my head made itself felt anew. I stared straight ahead, kept my eyes fixed, and gazed at the chemist's under the sign of the elephant. Hunger was waging a fierce battle in me at this moment, and I was suffering greatly. Whilst I sit thus and look out into space, a figure becomes little by little clear to my fixed stare. At last I can distinguish it perfectly plainly, and I recognize it. It is that of the cake-vendor who sits habitually near the chemist's under the sign of the elephant. I give a start, sit half-upright on the seat, and begin to consider. Yes, it was quite correct—the same woman before the same table on the same spot! I whistle a few times and snap my fingers, rise from my seat, and make for the chemist's. No nonsense at all! What the devil was it to me if it was the wages of sin, or well-earned Norwegian huckster pieces of silver from Kongsberg? I wasn't going to be abused; one might die of too much pride....

I go on to the corner, take stock of the woman, and come to a standstill before her. I smile, nod as to an acquaintance, and shape my words as if it were a foregone conclusion that I would return sometime.

"Good-day," say I; "perhaps you don't recognize me again."

"No," she replied slowly, and looks at me.

I smile still more, as if this were only an excellent joke of hers, this pretending not to know me again, and say:

"Don't you recollect that I gave you a lot of silver once? I did not say anything on the occasion in question; as far as I can call to mind, I did not; it is not my way to do so. When one has honest folk to deal with, it is unnecessary to make an agreement, so to say, draw up a contract for every trifle. Ha, ha! Yes, it was I who gave you the money!"

"No, then, now; was it you? Yes, I remember you, now that I come to think over it...."

I wanted to prevent her from thanking me for the money, so I say, therefore, hastily, whilst I cast my eye over the table in search of something to eat:

"Yes; I've come now to get the cakes."

She did not seem to take this in.

"The cakes," I reiterate; "I've come now to get them—at any rate, the first instalment; I don't need all of them today."

"You've come to get them?"

"Yes; of course I've come to get them," I reply, and I laugh boisterously, as if it ought to have been self-evident to her from the outset that I came for that purpose. I take, too, a cake up from the table, a sort of white roll that I commenced to eat.

When the woman sees this, she stirs uneasily inside her bundle of clothes, makes an involuntary movement as if to protect her wares, and gives me to understand that she had not expected me to return to rob her of them.

"Really not?" I say, "indeed, really not?" She certainly was an extraordinary woman. Had she, then, at any time, had the experience that some one came and gave her a heap of shillings to take care of, without that person returning and demanding them again? No; just look at that now! Did she perhaps run away with the idea that it was stolen money, since I slung it at her in that manner? No; she didn't think that either. Well, that at least was a good thing—really a good thing. It was, if I might so say, kind of her, in spite of all, to consider me an honest man. Ha, ha! yes indeed, she really was good!

But why did I give her the money, then? The woman was exasperated, and called out loudly about it. I explained why I had given her the money, explained it temperately and with emphasis. It was my custom to act in this manner, because I had such a belief in every one's goodness. Always when any one offered me an agreement, a receipt, I only shook my head and said: No, thank you! God knows I did.

But still the woman failed to comprehend it. I had recourse to other expedients—spoke sharply, and bade a truce to all nonsense. Had it never happened to her before that any one had paid her in advance in this manner? I inquired—I meant, of course, people who could afford it—for example, any of the consuls? Never? Well, I could not be expected to suffer because it happened to be a strange mode of procedure to her. It was a common practice abroad. She had perhaps never been outside the boundaries of her own country? No? Just look at that now! In that case, she could of course have no opinion on the subject; ... and I took several more cakes from the table.

She grumbled angrily, refused obstinately to give up any more of her stores from off the table, even snatched a piece of cake out of my hand and put it back into its place. I got enraged, banked the table, and threatened to call the police. I wished to be lenient with her, I said.

Were I to take all that was lawfully mine, I would clear her whole stand, because it was a big sum of money that I had given to her. But I had no intention of taking so much, I wanted in reality only half the value of the money, and I would, into the bargain, never come back to trouble her again. Might God preserve me from it, seeing that that was the sort of creature she was.... At length she shoved some cakes towards me, four or five, at an exorbitant price, the highest possible price she could think of, and bade me take them and begone. I wrangled still with her, persisted that she had at least cheated me to the extent of a shilling, besides robbing me with her exorbitant prices. "Do you know there is a penalty for such rascally trickery," said I; "God help you, you might get penal servitude for life, you old fool!" She flung another cake to me, and, with almost gnashing teeth, begged me to go.

And I left her.

Ha! a match for this dishonest cake-vendor was not to be found. The whole time, whilst I walked to and fro in the market-place and ate my cakes, I talked loudly about this creature and her shamelessness, repeated to myself what we both had said to one another, and it seemed to me that I had come out of this affair with flying colours, leaving her nowhere. I ate my cakes in face of everybody and talked this over to myself.

The cakes disappeared one by one; they seemed to go no way; no matter how I ate I was still greedily hungry. Lord, to think they were of no help! I was so ravenous that I was even about to devour the last little cake that I had decided to spare, right from the beginning, to put it aside, in fact, for the little chap down in Vognmandsgade—the little lad who played with the paper streamers. I thought of him continually—couldn't forget his face as he jumped and swore. He had turned round towards the window when the man spat down on him, and he had just looked up to see if I was laughing at him. God knows if I should meet him now, even if I went down that way.

I exerted myself greatly to try and reach Vognmandsgade, passed quickly by the spot where I had torn my drama into tatters, and where some scraps of papers still lay about; avoided the policeman whom I had amazed by my behaviour, and reached the steps upon which the laddie had been sitting.

He was not there. The street was almost deserted—dusk was gathering in, and I could not see him anywhere. Perhaps he had gone in. I laid the cake down, stood it upright against the door, knocked hard, and hurried away directly. He is sure to find it, I said to myself; the first thing he will do when he comes out will be to find it. And my eyes grew moist with pleasure at the thought of the little chap finding the cake.

I reached the terminus again.

Now I no longer felt hungry, only the sweet stuff I had eaten began to cause me discomfort. The wildest thoughts, too surged up anew in my head.

Supposing I were in all secrecy to cut the hawser mooring one of those ships? Supposing I were to suddenly yell out "Fire"? I walk farther down the wharf, find a packing-case and sit upon it, fold my hands, and am conscious that my head is growing more and more confused. I do not stir; I simply make no effort whatever to keep up any longer. I just sit there and stare at the Copégoro, the barque flying the Russian flag.

I catch a glimpse of a man at the rail; the red lantern slung at the port shines down upon his head, and I get up and talk over to him. I had no object in talking, as I did not expect to get a reply, either.

I said:

"Do you sail tonight, Captain?"

"Yes; in a short time," answered the man. He spoke Swedish.

"Hem, I suppose you wouldn't happen to need a man?"

I was at this instant utterly indifferent as to whether I was met by a refusal or not; it was all the same to me what reply the man gave me, so I stood and waited for it.

"Well, no," he replied; "unless it chanced to be a young fellow."

"A young fellow!" I pulled myself together, took off my glasses furtively and thrust them into my pocket, stepped up the gangway, and strode on deck.

"I have no experience," said I; "but I can do anything I am put to. Where are you bound for?"

"We are in ballast for Leith, to fetch coal for Cadiz."

"All right," said I, forcing myself upon the man; "it's all the same to me where I go; I am prepared to do my work."

"Have you never sailed before?" he asked.

"No; but as I tell you, put me to a task, and I'll do it. I am used to a little of all sorts."

He bethought himself again.

I had already taken keenly into my head that I was to sail this voyage, and I began to dread being hounded on shore again.

"What do you think about it, Captain?" I asked at last. "I can really do anything that turns up. What am I saying? I would be a poor sort of chap if I couldn't do a little more than just what I was put to. I can take two watches at a stretch, if it comes to that. It would only do me good, and I could hold out all the same."

"All right, have a try at it. If it doesn't work, well, we can part in England."

"Of course," I reply in my delight, and I repeated over again that we could part in England if it didn't work.

And he set me to work....

Out in the fjord I dragged myself up once, wet with fever and exhaustion, and gazed landwards, and bade farewell for the present to the town—to Christiania, where the windows gleamed so brightly in all the homes.

THE END

Made in the USA
Monee, IL
28 August 2023